Wendy St‹

Wendy Steele is author, wise woman, goddess. She is writer, dance teacher, mother and healer.

Magic is Wendy's passion. 'The Lilith Trilogy' leads the reader along the paths of the witches Qabalah, following Angel Parson's story of betrayal, retribution and redemption. Her magical story contains high magic as well as pagan ritual. 'The Standing Stone Book Series' focuses on the lives of three women linked together across time and space by the standing stone. The countryside is the focus of their magic, embracing the gods and goddesses, tree spirits, elves and fairies.

Wendy's latest writing is witchlit. Like chicklit, Lizzie Martin, her female protagonist is a modern woman, juggling work, family and a love life, often with humorous consequences.

You can hear Wendy telling her short stories in Pan's Grotto on her Welsh riverbank, on her YouTube channel, *The Phoenix and the Dragon.*

Wendy lives in Wales with her partner, Mike, and cats. If she's not writing or teaching dance, you'll find her renovating her house, clearing her land or sitting on her riverbank, breathing in the beauty of nature.

Please visit wendysteele.com for more info.

Also by Wendy Steele

Destiny of Angels
First Book in The Lilith Trilogy

Wrath of Angels
Second Book in The Lilith Trilogy

Too Hot for Angels
Six (eXtra Sexy) Extended Scenes
(The Lilith Trilogy)

Turn Down The Heat
A Short Story Anthology

Into The Flames
A Short Story Anthology

The Standing Stone - Home For Christmas
First Novella in The Standing Stone Series

The Standing Stone – Silence Is Broken
Second Novella in The Standing Stone Series

The Standing Stone – The Gathering
Third Novella in The Standing Stone Series

Wendy Woo's Year - A Pocketful of Smiles
101 ideas for a happy year and a happy you
(non-fiction)

The Naked Witch

A
Wendy Woo Witch Lit
novel

Wendy Steele

PHOENIX &
THE DRAGON

www.wendysteele.com

For Jasmine, with love xx

1

Elizabeth Martin splashed through the puddles in her new Wellington boots. She chose the luminous frog design herself. After four days of continuous rain, the drains were overflowing. Cars trundled down the high street sending waves flooding the pavements but Lizzie didn't care. In her waterproof trousers and coat, she peeped from beneath her fur lined hood at the host of disgruntled humanity making their way to work. She arrived at Brown, Melchett and Brown as black clouds deposited another downpour on the town.

"Morning!" Lizzie lowered her hood and smiled at Louise, the security guard on the desk.

"Morning, Liz." She nodded as Lizzie waved her security pass, extricated from the pocket of her plastic, paisley rucksack. "Not looking good for the Fayre tomorrow."

"Getting it out of its system. All be gone by home time!"

Louise shook her head, her raven black bob swivelling around her head. "You're too bloody cheerful."

"Sorry, weather's been getting to me too. Trying to lighten the mood." Lizzie leant an arm on the desk. "Rowan's latest crush has turned into an obsession and the hens have stopped laying." She lowered her voice. "Something's on its way, change is coming, I can feel it."

"Get on with you." Louise brushed her away with a grin. "I love you, Lizzie but that heavens stuff is bullshit."

"Whatever you say but it made you smile."

With a lighter heart and the desire for coffee bubbling through her system, Lizzie walked to the lift oblivious to the footprints she left on the marble floor. She wrestled her auburn curls from her hood and ran a finger over each eyebrow before the shiny lift doors opened.

With her waterproofs hanging up to dry in the cloakroom, Lizzie donned her work attire. Today purple velvet fell sumptuously to the floor from her waist. Yesterday it was navy blue, Wednesday was red and Tuesday was turquoise. Monday had been her 'Maid Marion' dress sewn in soft green cotton, a warm start to the week before the storm began. A round necked, organic cotton long sleeved top hugged her generous curves, while a jacket of rich velvet hung loosely from her shoulders. Today's headband glistened turquoise and green. She looked in the mirror. Jade eyes stared back at her and she shut them. Three deep breaths and three long exhales later, Lizzie opened her eyes and winked at her reflection.

Lizzie made her way to reception, her cheery 'good morning' extracting the usual mumbles in return. Six months into her probationary period at Brown, Melchett and Brown, Solicitors, Lawyers and Conveyancers since 1876, she knew better than to expect more. She enjoyed her job, sitting peacefully in her world behind the headphones, letting her fingers type at the commands of her ears. A few times a day, members of the public or clients with appointments would intrude but she helped them, offered drinks, guided them to their destinations and felt better for it. She had little to do with the main office.

When Suzanne came to relieve her, she liked to take her lunch to the park, where the squirrels waited for her, eager for a gift from her nut jar, once she'd sprinkled a good handful on her boxed salad. The last few days, as the rain poured down, she'd retreated to the bandstand where the squirrels found her beneath the cracking green paint and ornate wrought iron.

Stacks of folders, three bulbous towers, dwarfed her desk. Refraining from the sigh almost passing her lips, Lizzie removed the folders to the floor behind her. Ignoring the in-tray, already awash with paper, she pulled back her chair. Post cascaded off it like a cream soda fountain. Last night had been Rowan's Options Evening so Lizzie had taken two hours flexi time to make certain she would be there. The office, it seemed, had conspired to go into overdrive in her absence.

Pottering between the printer and her desk, Lizzie hummed a favourite chant. The office door flung back, a balding, rotund figure striding through the opening. He slammed two folders on the corner of Lizzie's desk, the damp shoulders of his jacket dark and steaming.

"Flamin' June? My arse!"

"Morning, Tom. Bad journey?"

"Slow and crowded. Lizzie, be a poppet and get me a coffee, would you? Suzanne isn't in yet."

Lizzie placed the frothing cup on the broad oak desk. Thomas Melchett emerged from his private bathroom, flattening the remainder of his hair to his head. His grey suit was creased and a mustard stain visible on his tie.

"You're an angel. Perfect. Thank you."

Back at her desk, Lizzie's nimble fingers raced across the keyboard. She admitted Tom's client, closely followed by one for David Brown, the other senior partner. His client was a much older man whose small dark eyes stabbed the world from beneath looming, monstrous eyebrows. He'd refused the seat she offered and insisted David be summoned immediately. He hovered at her desk while she called Tania, David's secretary. David arrived in reception, steering the man to his office with an arm on his elbow.

An hour later, a message flashed on Lizzie's screen. All staff were to assemble in the boardroom at 3pm. Lizzie smiled. Who had told them it was her birthday?

The rain eased and Lizzie chatted to the squirrels, seated on a bin liner beneath the oak tree. It dripped a bit through the leaves, but she enjoyed the sensation of her back against the ancient trunk. The squirrels wished her 'happy birthday', accepted a nut each and vanished. Single weighty raindrops hit the surface of the lake and Lizzie struggled into her coat. In moments, a great wet curtain soaked the park. Hurrying back to the office, Lizzie's hood flew back, her hair loose but she left it, shocked by the force of the rain on her scalp but exhilarated by its power.

4

With a mug of hot chocolate on her desk, she opened her drawer, taking out a slab of dark chocolate, a gift from Rowan this morning. Fourteen was a tumultuous age, Lizzie remembered, and often difficult not to behave like a rude cow but Rowan could be thoughtful. She savoured the taste as the rich chocolate coated her mouth.

The boardroom was not festooned with balloons and no cries of 'Happy Birthday!' greeted her entrance. Biting her lip, she forced back the blush threatening to bring tears and sidled over to Suzanne and two other secretaries, huddled by a table of drinks. No one was drinking.

"What's this all about?" she whispered.

Scared looks preceded shaking heads. "Neil reckons there's been a buyout. Sanderson Greybolt, he reckons."

"We'll have to move to London!"

"Not if we lose our jobs."

"Suz! Can't be that bad and, anyway, Neil doesn't know everything."

"What about the client, the man who came in before lunch. I didn't see him go, did you Suz? Tania?" They shook their heads at Lizzie.

"He's not a client." Tania's orange face winced and she glanced over her shoulder. Spidery lashes captured frightened blue eyes. "He's Mr Brown, the Mr Brown."

Suzanne and Chloe gasped.

"Who?" asked Lizzie.

5

"My uncle, Edward Brown, will be taking up a position at the firm here in Romford, from next week. This firm will be Brown, Melchett *and* Brown again."

David Brown wore a smile for a glimmer before a nervous tick took over his pale, flushed face. Sepia curls adhered cherub-like to his scalp but his large hooked nose and hooded eyes were not a bit angelic. Tania said he was fair but humour wasn't high on his list of acquired skills.

"So let's raise a toast to having the family together again!"

The staff sipped politely as Edward Brown stepped forward. "David's father and I dragged this company from the gutter in 1978 with the help of our friend, James Melchett, Thomas' father. We had standards then and we have them now. I've been through the books, which are none of your business but also your staff records, which are. Be assured, you will all retain your positions…"

An audible sigh trickled through the room.

"…while each of you is re-interviewed for your job. Only the best at Brown, Melchett and Brown, only the best."

By the time Lizzie walked home from the bus stop, her coat had lived up to its waterproof claims but her feet were wet and her knees were soggy. Thin slits had grown into splits around the ankles of her pretty but impractical boots. The driving rain in' her face had chilled her so she turned up the thermostat in the hall and dried the front of her hair as the heating clicked on.

"You in, Rowan?" She called up the stairs.

"No!"

Sat at the kitchen table, Lizzie sipped her coffee and opened her book. She would cook dinner at her own convenience tonight. The words jumped and shuddered on the page, refusing to be understood, her mind unable to focus. She stared at the three cards on the table. Rowan's was a drawing of a black cat with a wide grin, painted in acrylics on cardboard. The other two displayed an abundance of garish, pink flowers, cascading over a wall from Lizzie's mother and a single rose in a vase from her ex mother-in-law. The neat even handwriting in the former wished her daughter a happy day and delivered the obligatory single kiss.

With self-pity rising in her stomach, Lizzie dashed to the front door, bravely sticking out her head as she wrestled with the mail box. Junk mail and a postcard for Rowan from her father from New Zealand were the only soggy items.

Lizzie hummed as she chopped vegetables and sliced the tofu she had marinated overnight. Under the grill, she warmed two vegeburgers. Nothing stopped Rowan complaining about her cooking, not even her birthday, so pre-empting an argument seemed a good plan. Thunder interrupted her unpleasant musing, whether she would have a job, this time next week or not.

"Any plans for this weekend?"

"Well, I'm not seeing Dad, am I? Six weeks! How can anybody go on holiday for six weeks?"

Lizzie shook her head. She often did this while talking about Rowan's father. It stopped her saying what she thought. Rowan idolised her father, though she'd seen him only sporadically for the ten years they had been apart. There had been only two phone calls since last summer. He was a life coach and motivational speaker, travelling the world, selling his books and lifestyle which Rowan thought was cool. Lizzie knew he had stolen most of his ideas from her. He was a liar, cheat and fraud but Rowan needed to find out for herself. She did her best to protect her daughter but Rowan was a young woman who needed to find her own way. At present, Joshua Martin was holidaying at Mount Manganui with his latest girlfriend, Bryony. Lizzie knew Rowan relished the idea of this enhanced, fashionable blond being her stepmother and dreamed of shopping together and trips to the coffee shop while Lizzie saw the blinkered adoration of a needy woman who'd fallen for the Josh Martin charm. She didn't blame Bryony. It had been her, fifteen years ago.

"Do you fancy coming to the Charity Fayre with me?"

"In this?" Rowan's brown hair, vibrant with russet tones, swished back from her shoulders as she gesticulated towards the kitchen window, resounding with incessant rain.

"It'll be fine tomorrow."

"Maybe."

They ate their stir fry, Rowan happy with her burgers and the vegetables she chose to eat. Lizzie didn't mind. There were plenty to choose from. The chocolate fudge cake to follow was delicious, a treat from the bakery. They washed and dried up together.

"Thanks for this."

"No worries. Did you get anything from work?"

Lizzie froze. "Err, what do you mean?"

"Cards, flowers, you know."

Lizzie breathed and resumed sloshing in the sink. "No, no one knew it was my birthday. I don't know any of them well."

"Why don't you go out with them? You said they go out Friday lunchtimes and they play darts after work on a Thursday."

Lizzie shrugged. "I'm not good at making friends."

"You're like a hermit!"

"I'm not! Anyway, I've not been there long. I prefer to get to know people before I get too friendly. Remember, it was a big change for me, moving house, getting a new job so you'd be able to walk to school."

"Oh right, so it's my fault you haven't any friends!" Rowan threw the tea towel on the drainer.

"No! I…"

Rowan was already stomping up the stairs.

It was past ten in the evening. Rowan was quiet in her room, homework completed, hopefully. Lizzie eased into her waterproof coat and crept out the back door. She checked the bolts on the chicken run and walked the perimeter, checking for signs of intrusion or the future prospect of it. She couldn't cope with a blood bath in the morning.

9

At the bottom of the garden, she squeezed past the oak and rowan trees and opened an old wooden door. Smells of pine, incense and wet wool greeted her. Rowan called it her 'Mum Cave'. Lizzie called it Sanctuary. Neither carefully synchronised calendars nor lists adorned the walls. No colour co-ordinated work outfits or labelled files filled the cupboards. Swathed in rich tapestries and layers of ancient rugs, Lizzie's escape was the home she longed for. An ancient chaise longue, draped in rugs and throws spread along one wall. The corner opposite held an exquisite, dust free altar. In the centre sat a curvaceous wooden figure of the goddess.

She lit the candle, clasped between the arms of the goddess and flicked off her torch. Throwing herself onto the heap on the chaise longue, Lizzie sobbed, burying herself beneath her memories. Ten years. She'd gladly changed her life for Rowan, raising her with scant fatherly support, financial or otherwise but some days, she wished her life were different. The move had scared her, leaving a community who knew her and respected the quiet, gentle woman in the brightly coloured clothes. This new area was big, 1930s houses backing onto a vast 1970s estate. Mr Brody next door was kind, reminding her of her father in his smart trousers and blazer. She missed her Dad, but not his drinking. She didn't blame her mother for moving on with her life but now her father was dead, she wished they could talk about the happy times, but Mrs McCartney wanted the slate wiped. All evidence of her early childhood had been trashed when her father died. Only two photo albums and a small box of video and cine films remained, prised from her mother's hands by a fourteen year old Lizzie, sobbing as her childhood turned to ash.

Lizzie wept harder. And after all her efforts, all the planning and hard work, the job she loved was in jeopardy. She cuffed her eyes and extracted a tissue box from the desk. One day, she would have time to paint at that desk. One day. She blew her nose. Enough self-pity. The Charity Fayre was tomorrow and she had work to do.

She threw a large cushion on the floor and facing the altar, plonked herself, cross legged upon it. She drew her protection around her, evoking her favourite standing stones, and called in the goddess, to have a word about the weather.

2

A 9am alarm was a luxury and Lizzie wiggled her toes in bliss beneath the duvet. Sleep had eluded her for many hours when she returned from the garden. Finally drifting off, she dreamed of a woman with red hair in a navy suit, strolling down office corridors in impossibly high shoes.

Arriving at the park at 11am, Lizzie was greeted by watery sunshine and the steaming roof of the bandstand. She dropped a handful of nuts beneath the oak tree before following the muted sounds of a PA system across the park. She had volunteered to help set up the stall with Lou, selling cakes for her chosen charity, the local children's hospice. Lou had requested all her friends and the bowling group, to bake cakes for her to sell. Other stall holders were setting up, local wildlife groups, youth projects and women's groups, all hoping to further their personal causes under the banner of the Charity Fayre. Two men with brooms swept water from the bandstand, ready for live music from local bands to be played all afternoon.

Louise greeted her with a hug, gratefully accepting the tins of cakes Lizzie offered. They covered the stall in red plastic table cloths and managed to fashion a small awning to go over it, though it wouldn't withstand more than a light shower. At midday, with a small crowd gathered, the mayor opened proceedings, her heavy gold chain glinting in the ever brightening sunshine.

"You fixed this, did you?"

Louise pointed to the sun as they uncovered the cake stands and began to sell, popping cakes into paper bags and accepting cash with a smile.

"Of course."

"You're a weird one, no mistake, but I like you, all the same."

"Thanks, glad I'm not too weird for you. You're alright. I might even buy you a cup of tea later."

The stall sold out in an hour. The first band struck up and Lizzie fetched the promised tea. They sat on damp stripy deckchairs until Louise had to go.

"I promised Terry I'd join him bowling tonight. There's a big match on…well, big for them. Top ten team coming over from Loughton. You want to join us for a drink?"

"Thanks but I'm having a mummy and daughter night in."

"I thought Rowan might come today."

"She wasn't up when I left. Said she was tired."

"Another time then. Bowling's fun, honest. You and Rowan should go."

"Thanks, Lou. I might suggest it."

The band played on. Lizzie tried to decide the genre. It wasn't rock but it wasn't pop either, the words were too poetic for that. The lead singer was slim and fair, his thick hair restrained by a band at the nape of his neck. Lizzie watched his soft lips and stubbled chin as the poignant words seeped into her subconscious. The crowd grew, the beat picked up by the band until drums, bass and lead guitar filled the park with thrashing yet co-ordinated sound. The band took their bow to resounding applause, Lizzie joining in. The leaflet on the seat beside her informed her they were called Revenge is Sweet.

In her patchwork festival trousers and shoe string vest, Lizzie made a circuit around the stalls. There were limited resources in her purse but she wanted to make her contribution. A sweet gentle breeze kept her cool, as did the soft cotton wrap she threw about her shoulders so with the sun glinting off her hair, she indulged in a spot of fun. She bought a pair of black fingerless gloves; hand knitted by the local WI and a raffle ticket from the local wildlife group to win a bird box and an eco-stall, to win a water butt.

At the coconut shy, Lizzie took aim with the first of her three wooden balls. Uniformed scouts watched, smirking. It had been a difficult week. Rowan's obsession with a lower sixth form boy had reached a new level. Lizzie saw the email on Rowan's laptop as she trawled the floor and surfaces in her bedroom for dirty washing. Her ex-husband, Josh and his young girlfriend Bryony were lazing in a trendy New Zealand surfing resort. She hadn't picked up a sketch book all week. She had worked hard at her job. She could lose her job next week.

A satisfying crack resounded through the park and the first coconut bounced onto the grass. The crowd around her cheered. She took aim, her arm pulled back like a javelin thrower. The second coconut fell, the crowd roared and Lizzie pictured Josh's face on the third coconut. The ball spun from her hand. The force of the contact shattered the target.

Lizzie placed her prizes into her string bag with her new gloves.

"You've a cracking right arm, excuse the pun."

Lizzie looked up. "Thanks. I enjoyed your set."

It was the man's turn to blush. "Thanks but it could've been a lot tighter. We've only been back playing together a few months and it shows. I was on my way for coffee. Would you like one?"

No, run away, now, quick. "I'd love a tea."

"I'm Lizzie."

"Matt, shall we sit here?"

Lizzie and Matt lazed beside the lake in the sunshine. Strains of music tickled their ears from the bandstand. Ducks on the lake paraded their babies. Red faced children played with balloons, buried their faces in candy floss and cried, in turn.

"So you used to live around here?"

"Born and brought up in Gidea Park but I moved closer to the City. An apartment in the Docklands."

"So what brought you back? Sorry, you don't have to say."

Matt waved away her apology. "It's no big deal. My marriage ended and even with no children, I managed to lose my flat. I'm back living in the family home. Mum's gone to live in Spain with her boyfriend."

"Cool, house to yourself."

Matt bit his bottom lip and shook his head. "My father has business this way and has moved himself in. Cramped my style a bit."

"I wouldn't live with my mother if you paid me!"

"You live alone then?"

"With my daughter."

"Matt! Matt!"

They looked towards the bandstand to a figure in a top hat gesticulating wildly.

"I have to go."

"Me too."

"I don't have a card on me..." He hunted in the back pocket of his jeans. "I...can I call you, I mean, would you..."

No! Stop now! "Yes!" Lizzie extracted a pen from her bag and Matt offered a smooth forearm. Lizzie's knees wobbled, her fingers tingling at the feel of his soft warm skin.

Lizzie walked from the bus stop, skipping a little. It must have been the impetus exerted by the swinging bag of coconuts. It had nothing to do with spending half an hour, drinking tea beside a lake with a handsome man. It was past five o'clock and her stomach rumbled but she'd been nourished by a good day in good company and was looking forward to her evening with Rowan. Tonight's video choice was 'Grease', perfect viewing to sit in a face pack in pyjamas and sing along to. At the moment, Rowan enjoyed a musical and Lizzie hoped it would last.

The side gate swung open in the breeze as Lizzie approached her house so she entered that way, bolting the gate behind her.

Rowan leapt up from a man's lap as Lizzie walked into the kitchen.

"Hi, Mum!"

She lay back on the chaise longue in her Sanctuary, clasping her hot water bottle to her chest. Her heart pounded in her ears while her head recapped the past five hours. All evening, she had appeared calm and composed while inside she was screaming, 'Stay away from my daughter!' Sam was pleasant, amiable, blond and cute and he fronted a band. She understood why Rowan liked him but what did a young man of almost eighteen see in her daughter?

Lizzie relaxed back into the blankets, a single candle lighting the wooden cabin with a delicate peachy light. A vision of her daughter's face fixed on the object of her adoration made Lizzie squirm. But Rowan wasn't a baby any more. She had wanted to ban her from seeing Sam, wrap her in cotton wool and keep her safe from the big bad world but she didn't. Instead, she'd looked Sam square in the eyes and told him she preferred to be around if they were in the house. She saw Rowan's annoyance, frustration creasing her brow but Sam smiled and nodded and agreed. They drank tea. Sam left and mother and daughter enjoyed their evening together.

It had been a good day. The sun had shone, the Charity Fayre had been a success and both mother and daughter had fallen for the lead singer of a band.

3

Lizzie sat sipping her tea, watching her daughter eating muesli. It was Sunday and before 10am so Lizzie was intrigued. The phone rang in the hall and Rowan leapt like a gazelle and in three springs, had reached it. Lizzie smiled.

"It's for you." Rowan's eyebrows raised into her messy hair.

Lizzie ordered her feet not to hurry to the phone.

"Well?"

Lizzie sat and picked up her mug. "It was someone I met at the Fayre. You should have come. The weather was glorious and you'd have enjoyed the music."

"Someone?"

"Yes and the sun is out again and I'm going for a walk. Do you want to come?"

"Nah, you're alright."

Lizzie gathered tissues and keys into her bag. "I meant what I said last night."

"I know! Why do you have to go on?" Rowan slammed her mug on the kitchen table, hot chocolate spattering the surface.

Lizzie brought a cloth. "I'm sorry but be patient with me, Rowan. Last time I looked, you loved Little Ponies and wore your hair in bunches!"

Rowan tried not to smile. "I get it but you can trust me."

19

"I know." She wanted to believe it. She really did.

She'd promised herself she would take things slowly but less than half way round the lake, she clung to Matt's arm, relishing the relaxed company. She met his blue eyes and smiled. Beneath her favourite oak, they ate the crusty rolls, goats' cheese and apples she had brought and sipped old fashioned ginger beer. They laughed about flared trousers. Matt was two years older than her and they reminisced about kids' television programmes and the rise of celebrities.

As the sun passed its zenith, Matt asked her who she worked for. It may have been her lack of sleep or the kindness of his words but in seconds, Lizzie was sobbing into his shoulder.

She grabbed for her bag and a tissue. "I'm so sorry. What must you think of me?" She blew her nose loudly.

"There's obviously a problem. Why don't you tell me about it?"

"We've only just met and now you know what a soggy mess I am." Did I really say that out loud? Idiot.

"Come here." Matt drew her to him and she breathed in expensive aftershave and warm man.

Lizzie told him about the arrival of Edward Brown.

"But you're bound to pass the interview. You've never had a warning or any disciplinary action?"

"No, of course not but Edward Brown said he wanted 'the best'. I don't know if I am the best." Oh, you pathetic puppy.

"Of course you are but what about the other staff? Any of them likely to go?"

"You're right! I've been so selfish! Suzanne is recently engaged and Tania's a big mortgage to pay."

"I meant had anyone been warned, you know, for not adhering to their contract?"

Lizzie stared, red eyed at Matt's intense face. "How would I know?"

"No, well, sorry, I was trying to make you feel your job was perhaps safer than others which is mean, sorry."

She watched his soft lips, tripping over his words and her shoulders relaxed. She blew her nose again. "There's no point me worrying anyway. I'll have my interview and the firm will decide. Nothing I can do."

Matt put his arm around her shoulder and squeezed her arm. "Sorry, all the waiting must be grim. Do you want to walk?"

"Thanks but I should get home. I've a mound of laundry and I usually batch cook meals for the week." And now he knows what an exciting life you lead!

She arrived home with nuts in her pocket. She hadn't seen the squirrels all day.

Lizzie walked into the lounge to find Rowan behind the ironing board and a film blaring out from Netflix. She clung to the back of the sofa in surprise.

"Hi, Mum! Thought I'd make a start before it got too dry! How was your walk?"

Lizzie grabbed the remote control and paused the film.

"Good. You know I like to walk and think. Thanks for this."

"No worries and so you know, Sam came round."

Lizzie held her breath.

"I told him you were out and he was going to go but I hope it was okay to have a drink in the garden, Mum. He'd cycled from Emerson Park. He went straight after."

Lizzie breathed. "Of course it was okay, love. I would have done the same myself."

She busied in the kitchen, checking the soaked beans and putting them on to boil. "So where does his band play?"

Rowan stood iron in hand, her usually tanned face pale and her rich brown eyes staring. "You're not going to watch him play?"

4

"We raised almost a hundred and fifty and the event total was close to two thousand!"

"That's great news, Lou. I had a fun day."

Lizzie told her about the coconuts.

"You have to come bowling!"

"I think it's a slightly different technique." Lizzie smiled. "But Lou, your job's safe, isn't it?"

Louise face was puzzled. "I don't know any different, why?"

"Oh, nothing, shake-up at my firm. Glad it doesn't affect you."

"No, I'm security for the whole building, all four companies but you're not going to lose your job, are you? They need a smiling face on reception."

"Thanks for that but we're all being re-interviewed."

"What a cheek! Look, I'm off at five today, rather than six. My boss is training up new staff for a few hours. Do you fancy a cuppa or something stronger before you head home? I missed your birthday because someone didn't tell me!"

"Sorry. You know, I'd like that. I'll text Rowan and tell her I'll be a bit late. Thanks, Lou."

"No problem and you might have some news by then."

Lizzie ignored the stares in the wine bar. In her 'Maid Marion' dress they probably thought she was the cabaret. She sipped eagerly on her white wine spritzer.

"I'm glad you told me about your job, Liz. Any news on your interview"

"Wednesday. They told me I had to be ready for Wednesday. What does that mean? Ready for what?"

"I don't know hun but I have to be re-interviewed too."

"Why?"

"Seems the whole building is having a shake-up. Tess from Acorn Property told me."

"Could Edward Brown have anything to do with this?"

"Who's he?"

He arrived Friday morning and since then, everything is changing."

"Where's he been?"

"I have no idea. It was announced that he was back. David didn't say where from."

"But how could he be involved in the whole building changing their staff?"

Lizzie shook her head. "It seemed a coincidence, that's all."

"You and your coincidences!" Lou's lacquered bob shimmied around her head. "Companies are always looking for ways to save money, get the most from their staff. I'm not worried. I've been working that building for four years with no complaints. I'm sure you'll be fine too."

Lizzie sipped her drink. "I hope so, Lou. Not sure how I can keep my house otherwise."

Though Tuesday didn't bring more rain, the sky remained grey all day and the temperature rose as the trapped heat built up. Tempers reared in the office, staff snapping at her as she tried to keep cheerful. Even the usual relaxed journey home was spoiled by two passengers arguing over an open window. A toddler's grizzle became a howl at their raised voices and his incessant crying scraped at Lizzie's nerves.

Rowan wasn't back from drama club so once the slow cooker was checked, Lizzie hurried to the bottom of the garden. Spell weaving on a Tuesday in the middle of a moon cycle was new for her but the moon was waxing and Tuesday was ruled by Mars. She could do with as much strength, power and authority as she could muster.

Once her circle of protection was cast, she sat cross legged, clasping a thumbnail sized ruby. On the altar, a white candle burned and frankincense filled the cabin. She had called the angels to her for protection, seeking their support before the following day's ordeal.

> *"Uriel above me*
> *Michael beneath me*
> *Raphael to my left*
> *Gabriel to my right*
> *By the power of these great angels*
> *Surround me with light."*

She visualised the interview, she in her favourite purple skirt, sitting opposite the Brown's and Tom and them smiling happily, shaking her hand.

Lizzie and Rowan pushed the burned vegetable casserole around their plates. She should have turned the slow cooker off. She was tempted to heat up the emergency pizzas in the freezer but fought the urge. Would there be any money to replace them? She ate the carrots and beans and suggested Rowan did the same.

"It's a bit yuck."

"I know, sorry. The chickens will love it. How was drama?"

Rowan used her fork like a conductor's baton as she enthused. "It was brilliant! We've been improvising about the plague! Like, some of us were sick but trying not to show it, while Kelly and Lyn were mother and daughter and Kelly had to watch her die! Wicked!"

"And this is for what? Is there going to be a performance or something?"

"What do you mean 'for what'? It's about delving into people's feelings, into lives we can't imagine, about relationships, people and life. We don't learn someone else's script and recite on a stage like when you were at school!"

Harsh, that was harsh, Rowan but how could you know how old and tired I feel right now? "I'm trying to understand. Be kind."

"It's art, Mum! It isn't all about putting on a show for other people! You used to paint, right? So you paint your feelings. We act. It's about engaging with the subject, not planning a pretty play for other people!"

Lizzie nodded. "I can see that but the plague? Why the plague? Isn't that history?"

Rowan's eyes rolled to the ceiling and Lizzie wished she hadn't asked. "Illness and death isn't just history! It's incredibly relevant today and unless we feel, how can we sympathise? How can we empathise or interact with those who are dying? You know, for a painter, sometimes I don't think you've an artistic bone in your body!"

She could feel tiny cracks skittering across the armour she had built around herself. Rowan's thoughtless remarks didn't usually affect her so badly. The scary prospect of unemployment and the nagging worry of unpaid bills were playing on her mind. She would revisit the cabin before she went to bed but first, the remnants of their meal needed to be cleared. Rowan had taken the tin of flapjack to her room as Lizzie ran hot water. The phone rang in the hall. Rowan ran down the stairs to answer it. Five minutes later, she brought the cordless handset to Lizzie.

"It's Nanny Martin for you."

Lizzie dried her hands. "Hi, Marsha. Thanks for my card."

"You should have let me know it had arrived."

"Sorry, I was helping at a Charity…"

"How's Joshua?"

"Well, I imagine. He's holidaying in New Zealand with Bryony."

"I know but you don't know he's alright! I dreamed last night about a great white shark…"

Like her own mother, Marsha Martin was only in her early sixties but had failed to grasp that life moves on. Lizzie was once married to her son and was, therefore, part of the family, especially as she was the mother of

Marsha's only grandchild. On their first meeting, fifteen years ago, Lizzie had given her an insight into a recurring dream and had been her ear to help decipher them ever since. From her luxury villa near Ojen near Marbella, she peeked occasionally at the real world but preferred her own, surrounded by wealth and her devoted staff, including a young man called Antonio. Her second husband left her wealthy. She changed her name back to Martin, in honour of her son. Both women knew Josh only visited his mother when he wanted money.

"They don't have a shark problem in New Zealand, Marsha. Josh will be fine. And Bryony too."

"You're always so sure, so certain the best will happen! Maybe, you're right. I worry and the dreams are so vivid."

"I know you do, Marsha but I don't have any control over what Josh does any more. You know that."

"I've not met Bryony yet. Is she good for Josh?"

A sigh racked Lizzie's body loosening more cracks. "I've only met her once but she seems nice. I'm sure she makes Josh happy."

"Well, that's good. Rowan's missing him, she told me, poor love. If only you two could have worked it out."

Don't go there, please don't go there! "That's the past now, Marsha. Rowan and I are looking to the future. I went to her parents' evening about choosing options for school…"

"Must dash. Antonio is making his famous paella for us to enjoy by the pool this evening. I'll speak to you soon."

Lizzie held the receiver, staring at the dead black plastic, her eyes welling with pain and frustration.

It was past midnight. She entered through the wooden portal to the calming fragrance of frankincense. The goddess greeted her, her candle lit and Lizzie sat on the floor in her pyjamas and dressing gown and opened the cloth on the floor. The cards inside were dog eared but their message was always clear when she asked a question. Fear rumbled in her stomach as it always did when she shuffled her cards and prepared herself.

It was a simple spread. Sometimes she drew extra cards above each one to focus on the original but the cards this evening left no doubt of their meaning.

The past was IX Cups, nine golden goblets, a time of celebration and a time to ensure the creative potential of others. She remembered Rowan's birth, how young, excited and proud she and Josh had been of their new beautiful daughter but Lizzie had raised her. She had given her time to Rowan.

The present was VII Wands and the figure was Lizzie, fighting with her single club against the world, defiant and resolute against all odds. Once the divorce and the haggling were over, she had reinvented herself. Instead of fighting, she had turned to hard work. Practical, calm and organised, she had created a life that worked for her and Rowan.

The future was II Swords, a blindfolded figure beneath a crescent moon, bearing the weight of two mighty swords. Lizzie was confused and frightened beneath the burden of the swords she wielded yet, there was another fight ahead. Amidst the turmoil, an important decision would need to be made. An ally was what she needed. A friend she could trust.

Lizzie shut her eyes as a new day dawned, ruled by Mercurial dealings of communication, speaking, learning and teaching. She sent up a final prayer before trudging back to bed.

5

"Sam's band is playing on Saturday night at The Bitter End. It's the Battle of the Bands. Can I go?"

"It's a pub, Rowan. You know you can't."

Rowan shovelled in another spoonful of muesli. Her next words were muffled. "You could come."

"Sorry?"

"I said 'You could come'. Look, if it's the only way I can go, I'll chance it. Promise you'll stay at the back?"

"I haven't said 'yes' yet!"

"Please, Mum!"

"Can I think about it?"

"No, because you'll talk yourself out of it! It'll be a night out for you. Please!"

"Are they headlining?"

"No, it's different from a regular gig. Four bands have been invited. Playing order is drawn from a hat. They get a sound check then the music starts at eight o'clock, four half hour sets. Then we get to vote on the best band and the winner goes through to the next round."

Lizzie opened one of the three letters on the kitchen table. She recognised the handwriting as Aunt Matilda's, a maiden aunt of her father's. A crisp card, adorned with butterflies and glitter emerged and five shabby ten pound notes.

"Okay but you owe me."

On the bus to work, Lizzie tried to remember to breathe. Her mouth was dry and her head was light and muzzy. A text from Matt had suggested meeting up this evening but she'd cried off, offering Rowan up as her excuse. He suggested she made arrangements for Friday night. She promised to try.

The sun tried to shine on her as she walked from the bus stop but there were clouds to burn away. Lizzie wished she'd worn her purple skirt. She clung tightly to her turquoise sequined wrap, a chill breeze whipping through her second favourite dress, a floor length creation with a Cinderella hem in shades of turquoise, gold and purple.

Louise greeted Lizzie with a grin. "You look stunning! That colour with your hair is amazing. You should take up modelling."

Lizzie laughed. "I'm far too short and curvy for that but, thanks for the support."

Louise's smile faded. "Today's the day?"

Lizzie nodded.

"Me too."

Lizzie squeezed her friend's hand. "Good luck."

Lizzie waited for the lift. Her armour was intact and her sword sharpened. She hoped she wouldn't have to use it.

The three men sat in front of her, as she had visualised, with Chantelle from HR and Suzanne taking notes. Tom Melchett began with easy questions, taken from her CV. He turned to Edward Brown, reading the glowing praise for her work from him, David and other staff members.

"But she's still on probation?" queried Edward Brown.

Hello! I'm here!

"She is but I wouldn't hesitate to give her a permanent contract!"

"You wouldn't but I would. Mrs Martin, how do you like working for Brown, Melchett and Brown?"

Lizzie's prepared answer flowed from her tongue. She tried not to gush, not to let them know how important this job was to her. Edward Brown flicked pages in a folder as she spoke.

"And you think you're the best person to be on reception?"

Beneath the severe hooded brows, two black darts pierced through the air but they didn't penetrate Lizzie's armour.

"Now, yes. I know all the clients and have a good working relationship with the staff. I'm patient but tactful on the telephone. I'm professional and take pride in every aspect of my work."

Edward lowered his gaze and muttered.

"That'll be all for now, Lizzie. All staff will be notified on Monday morning."

"Monday?"

The word shot into the small stifling room before she could stop it. Five pairs of eyes stared at her.

"Something wrong, Mrs Martin?"

"No, not at all. Shall I make a tray of tea for you before your next interview?"

Lizzie hurried past Louise on her way to lunch. She waved a hand at Louise's worried face and ran through the door.

Lizzie sat beneath the oak tree. "Have these people no soul? Don't they understand how terrible it is to live in limbo like this?"

The squirrel shook his head sadly and accepted a nut. He sat back on his haunches and nibbled while Lizzie talked.

"It struck me as I walked out of that room, you know, what Rowan was talking about. You need to live a person's life to understand how they feel. If you care. David and Tom care, I think but Edward Brown…How can he walk into the company and do as he pleases? I was employed by David and Tom, not him!"

Two more squirrels approached followed by two more. Lizzie shared her worries with them all and her nuts and her salad sandwich.

"Sorry, Lou. I had to get out."

"You okay? How did it go?"

"Decision on Monday."

"Monday? Oh, Lizzie. They're telling security straight away. Everyone's okay so far and mine's in half an hour."

"You'll be fine."

"But what about you?"

Lizzie polished her armour. "I'll be fine until Monday."

She chose the Pasta Palace. If it came to paying her half, she could manage with her birthday money in her purse.

She wasn't hungry but Matt's handsome smiling face relaxed her. She'd been ready to burst from her armour all day.

The olives were good and the sauce on the pasta delicious. Lizzie smiled her first true grin of the day, sitting back in her chair, sipping ice cold spritzer.

"You should have told them! Monday is too long to wait to hear your future!"

"I couldn't and anyway, it's the same for all the staff. Everyone is suffering."

"Especially those who've black marks against them."

"Do you think? I know Tania had time off sick at the beginning of the year."

"Sick or shirking?"

"Sick, of course! She had to have a minor operation, poor girl but she's fine now. They wouldn't hold that against her, would they?"

Matt shrugged. "Probably not. I reckon it's more the people who've meddled where they shouldn't, you know. Broken a confidence or caused trouble for the company. Do you know anyone like that?"

Lizzie shook her head. "No, they're not like that. None of them."

"I thought you didn't know them well. That's what you said."

"No, but there's always rumours in an office. I've heard none." She sipped her drink and relaxed even more. "I have a good feeling around all of them."

"Feeling?"

"How I feel around them, the energy they give off. Sometimes they're confused or worried."

"You can sense that?"

Lizzie nodded.

"And the new boss, what's his name?"

"Edward Brown. He's guarded, hiding maybe but I don't spend much time with him."

"He's the new man, has to be careful."

"You're probably right."

"Dessert?"

"Not for me, thanks. You go for it."

Matt smiled, his large hand falling from his glass to cover Lizzie's small hand. "I finished your pasta, I'm done. Do you want to come back to mine for coffee?"

"Thanks but I want to get back. Rowan has two friends staying over."

Matt squeezed her hand, his eyes scanning her face as if she were a new, delightful, delicious creature he'd discovered. "I'm sure they'll be fine."

She took a deep breath. "I will be too, once I'm home." She rescued her hand and folded her napkin. "Thank you for a lovely evening."

6

Saturday morning dawned and Lizzie woke early to a lazy orange sun, spraying its beauty over the summer landscape. In short yellow dungarees, she gathered her garden tools into her trug and set about weeding the flower bed in the front garden. While the majority of garden was covered in easy maintenance gravel, peonies and honeysuckle fought for space in the bed behind the fence while forget-me-nots and pansies struggled for sunlight beneath them.

She was pulling stray grass and dandelions from the path when a black car pulled up to the kerb and two large feet approached. Lizzie looked up. The man wore jeans one size too big and a black t-shirt with skulls and dragons on the front. He held a piece of paper.

"Rowan Martin?"

Rowan leapt through the front door like a genie from its bottle, her back pack bulging. "Hi!"

The man viewed Rowan, his face puzzled. She'd plaited her thick brown hair, lifting it from her neck into a woven basket on her head. Wisps of curls fell against her face, a beautiful face, open and beaming and devoid of any make up.

"You ready?"

"Yup."

"Err, hello?"

Lizzie stood up.

"Hey, Mum. Have to go. Final band practise!"

"When will you be back?"

"I'm going with the band. I'll see you in The Bitter End at eight, if you're still coming."

Rowan and the man walked to the car. It was brand new. It had a Mercedes badge.

"Sorry, who are you?"

"Mum!"

The man turned and offered a hand. "Richard Parker, Sam's father."

Lizzie arrived before eight o'clock to strains of tuning and testing of microphones. Her short cotton shift dress was cool after the heat of the summer's hottest day so far but the bar was crowded, noisy and sweaty. She'd weeded in the back garden until it was too hot to work outside. Shopping, baking and cooking were complete. She could have a lie-in in the morning.

With her lime and water in her hand, she scanned the crowds for Rowan. Young men and women thronged around the front of the stage but she couldn't see her. She wandered to the back of the pub, past pool tables surrounded by eager young cocks, strutting their prowess before clucking little hens. In the chill out room, a room of three sides, open to the garden, in a haze of smoke, she found Rowan. Lizzie didn't approach but stood a moment to admire her daughter. While young women fawned and young men joshed around Sam and the band on a large sofa, Rowan was curled in a chair opposite with a book, sipping cola from a bottle through a straw.

At nine o'clock Walking Shadow took the stage. Lizzie stayed as far back as she could while still able to see Rowan. The band was tight. The rhythms were toe-tappingly good and Sam was an excellent front man. His big blond body owned the stage. The raw, earthy, guttural quality of his voice stroked her ears and his words were pertinent rather than sentimental.

"Thank you."

Lizzie turned to the voice at her ear. Her puzzled face caused Richard Parker to lean closer.

"For Rowan."

Lizzie shook her head and Richard beckoned her towards the pool tables. She glanced at Rowan, standing against the wall singing along with Sam and followed Richard.

"I'm sorry, I don't understand."

Richard had found two stools and they sat at a sticky wrought iron table.

"Your Rowan. She's great."

"Well, I know that but what's been happening between her and Sam?"

Tiny cracks sizzled over Lizzie's armour.

"Nothing, no nothing like that. Please, don't worry." Richard laid a gentle hand on her forearm. "Sam had to move schools, to take his 'A' levels and he struggled for months. Until he met Rowan. The other girls are…different or maybe Rowan is different from the other girls."

Lizzie sipped her drink. How could this man know something about her daughter that she didn't? "Like how?"

Richard grinned and his sad, pale face lit up. "Have you seen her?"

Lizzie smiled and nodded. "So?"

"I'll start at the beginning, if that's okay. I need a drink, would you like one?"

"Lime and sparkling water would be lovely."

"Of course."

"My wife died suddenly three years ago of a brain haemorrhage."

"I'm so sorry."

Richard acknowledged her apology. "I'm only telling you all this because we love our kids. You deserve to know who Rowan is hanging out with."

"I appreciate that but if it's too painful…"

"Eilidh not being here will always hurt, I know that but like I said, this is about Sam and Rowan. She's healing my son so, you deserve to know."

Lizzie smiled at the sad, pale face of a grieving man. "Thank you."

"Eilidh had a tough time delivering Sam. We were very young but were advised not to have any more children. Eilidh adored Sam but continued to study, completing her law degree and final exams for the bar. I was already in the force when he was born so we brought Sam up together, spending precious time-off as a family. Maybe we did spoil him, buying him guitars and a drum kit and sound proofing the garage but he was always a good lad. When

Eilidh died, Sam changed. He played up to the sycophants hanging around the band, gave up on his school work and hated everyone and everything."

"Must have been devastating...for both of you."

Richard looked down. "There were days I didn't want to go on, I'll admit that but Sam was my major concern and I didn't know what to do to help him. And then Eilidh's will was read. She'd said she had money from an aunt when we met in college but it was never mentioned again. With Eilidh's inheritance, I bought the house in Emerson Park and moved Sam to a school excelling in the subjects he had originally been interested in. He hated me for six months. Until the day he bumped into your daughter in the library."

"Really? I'm intrigued but what about you? Do you still work?"

"Only in a consultancy capacity now. Detective work in London is an unpleasant business. I help, if I can but I'm happy to leave the fraud squad behind!"

The leather front seat moulded around her, safe and familiar as a comfy glove. Rowan and Sam bantered and laughed on the back seat behind her while Richard cruised them home. Both men left the car to see the women indoors, Lizzie blushing as Sam held Rowan's arms and kissed her forehead before giving her a hug.

"Thanks for the chat, Liz. I've not...well, it's not something I care to share with just anybody."

"It's been nice to meet you too. Thanks for the lift home."

"You up for tomorrow, Rowan?"

Rowan looked at Lizzie. "Sam's helping me organise my art project for next year. Can he come here as I've books from the library?"

"Of course. I'll have my usual Sunday walk but you two can manage. I've made a nut roast for dinner, if you want to stay, Sam?"

"Thanks, Mrs Martin. Can Dad come and get some cookery lessons?"

"Sam!"

Lizzie laughed. "Of course he can, though I'm not a great cook, Rowan will tell you. You're welcome to lunch, Richard. I'll be back by midday."

"I don't want to put you out…"

"You'd rather be on your own with your trains!"

The blush must have begun at Richard's toes as by the time it reached his face, he was bright red and squirming. "Thanks for that, son. Are you sure, Lizzie?"

Lizzie did her best to expel the image of Richard surrounded by a model train set, wearing a peaked cap and waving a tiny flag, from her mind. "Of course! See you tomorrow."

Lizzie and Matt had completed their circuit of the lake and were heading for the tea shop. The past few days revisited Lizzie's mind and she played out scenarios in her head. Most didn't end well or were based on other people behaving in certain ways, and that rarely happened.

"Band practise this afternoon. Want to come?"

"Sorry?"

"I wondered if you wanted to come to band practise later. I could croon you a ditty of your own, if you like."

Lizzie laughed and spun away from Matt's arm. The glorious summer weather beamed on the park today. With her sandals in her bag, Lizzie danced across the grass barefoot towards her oak tree and threw herself on the dry grass in front of it. The ancient trunk supported her.

"I thought you wanted tea."

Was that frustration in his voice? "Sorry, the moment took me. Sit here. It's beautiful in the shade."

"I'm getting a coffee."

Lizzie watched as Matt walked away. A squirrel appeared beside her. "Impatient, isn't he?"

The squirrel tipped his head to one side.

"Ah, it's probably me." She rummaged in the bottom of her bag and pulled out a few monkey nuts. She handed one to the squirrel.

"I feel…" Lizzie shut her eyes and tipped her head back against the ancient wood. "I feel I'm an observer on the world, squirrel. As if it's happening without me. I'm the flotsam, buffeted on the current of other people's lives."

She opened her eyes. Sunlight glinted through the lime green leaves, stencilling a pattern on her face and the earth.

"I brought you tea."

"Thank you. I'm sorry, Matt. I did say I wouldn't be good company."

"And I'm sorry too. I'm hot. Don't really fancy spending four hours in a metal garage, if I'm honest."

Lizzie laughed. "But you were going to subject me to it too!"

43

Matt smiled. "Because you're a breath of fresh air, little flower."

It's a compliment. He doesn't know. Matt, using her father's pet name for her, sent goose bumps down her spine.

Lizzie stood at the stove stirring gravy. Richard sat at the kitchen table.

"I didn't drink at all for years and then had a glass of wine at a wedding and realised what I'd been missing!" Lizzie laughed at the memory of her younger self, dancing all evening after three glasses of red wine.

"But it's understandable. If in your childhood, drink equalled hurt, why wouldn't you avoid it?"

"But then I decided that by avoiding a drink, if I wanted one of course, I was still allowing the past to affect me. Drink doesn't bother me now, not that I hang around drunks for recreation."

Richard smiled. "So what does bother you? Anything?"

Lizzie paused at her stirring, exploring every inch of the wooden spoon with her stare. She turned to Richard. "Right now, nothing. My daughter has planned her art project for next year and is getting excited about studying classics. I can hear her laughing in the garden. I've a tasty meal to look forward to in good company and I've a roof over my head." She picked up her gin and tonic from the counter and offered it up. "Cheers!"

"Cheers!"

"You learn anything, Dad?" Sam grinned.

"Of course, I'm perceptive at all times. Notes have been taken."

"Good because these roast potatoes are the best! Rowan! Don't move your feet!"

The faded green sun umbrella swayed above them before settling itself into the centre hole in the table. It needed four pairs of feet on the ill-fitting plastic base to keep the umbrella up but everyone agreed, dinner in the garden was a rare and enjoyable treat.

"Do you barbeque?" asked Richard.

"We've tried a few of the disposable ones but vegeburgers tend to disintegrate."

"Corn's good though, Mum but it takes ages."

"I forgot you were veggies. We'll need to clean up the barbeque before you come round!" Richard laughed.

"You can, Dad. It's not been used for years!"

"Thanks. Have you plans for the summer? You girls going abroad?"

"I might get to go to my Nan's in Spain, if my Dad gets organised but Mum doesn't come."

"We've had holidays in static caravans most years to Norfolk, Suffolk, Hampshire or Dorset. I…don't drive. Not anymore but I couldn't afford to run a car anyway. Buses are fine, coaches or trains. We've hired bikes for the week on the sites we've stayed on…"

"Do you remember the one with the little trailer behind?"

Lizzie laughed. "The trailer with the rain cover, I remember. Everywhere I rode, it rained until we got there and then the sun came out!"

"And one time, I got out and screamed because your mascara had run and I thought you were a zombie or something!"

Lizzie blushed and pulled her cotton throw onto her shoulders. Unlike most redheads, if careful, Lizzie's skin achieved a honey glow in the summer but she preferred to sit in the shade. Unlike her ex mother-in-law. Lizzie's offers of sun protection to Marsha had been met by guffaws, a noise usually confined to constipated donkeys.

"Kids never remember the memories you expect them to but the blessing is they don't remember the incidents we've spent sleepless nights agonising over. Parents make mistakes. We're not perfect, but we do our best," reassured Richard.

Lizzie and Richard smiled at each other. Rowans fingers went towards her mouth and executed the vomit sign.

"Oh, p-lease! Sam! Did you bring…you know?"

"Dad, keys. Sorry, Rowan. They're in the boot."

It was easy to extricate the bright green stalks from the river of floating strawberries. They poured the fruit from a jug onto soya ice cream, which had retained a little frost.

"I didn't know if you ate dairy as well."

"We do, we're veggie not vegan but I prefer the soya yoghurt and this ice cream's good."

"We went strawberry picking after practise. Richard's going to make jam." Rowan grinned at Sam's Dad as she delivered the final sentence.

"You're blushing like your strawberries, Dad."

"There is nothing wrong with a man learning to make jam! I don't like the stuff from the supermarket, okay? So I decided to learn to make my own and I shall do it tomorrow."

"Do you have enough jars?"

Richard's face contorted, Rowan giggled and Sam smirked. Lizzie glared at the children. "I am going to remove my feet and so is your Dad, Sam. We are going to the kitchen to discuss the finer points of jam making. Catch the brolly."

"That's a stunning dress. Have you always loved colour?"

"Thank you. Actually, no. There were times in my life that were grey and black."

"I'm sorry."

"Don't be. There has to be pain to be able to enjoy the pleasure, or something like that. After I split with Rowan's father, I brought the colour back."

"I sense only part way back."

Lizzie nodded. They sat on cushions and bits of foam on a picnic mat in the garden.

"I loved to paint as a child and…then I stopped. I painted when I met Josh and had Rowan…"

"And then you stopped but you've brought the colour back in other ways, with your clothes."

"Only partly. Do you know why I dress as I do?"

"Because you love colour?"

"No, not really. I like some colour. It's a kick in the teeth to the grey and black days but the main reason is, it's the only way I can afford to dress. Skirts, good quality second hand full skirts, I can alter. Velvet always looks good. Longer skirts mean you can get away with flat shoes, which are cheaper and far more practical for the amount of time I'm on my feet. A scrap of material or ribbon can make a headband or belt and change the look of an outfit completely. It feels good to create something for myself and I'm saving the planet."

"My Scottish grandmother would call you 'a canny wee thing'."

"I've survived. We've survived."

"It's a shame about the clothes though."

"Why?"

"No, none of my business, sorry."

"You have to say now, you started it!"

"I was going to say, a lot of people wear a mask, while you wear colourful armour."

Her heart skipped and her throat tightened. She gulped at her tea, allowing the gentle aroma and subtle taste to relax her.

Lizzie's green eyes held Richard's attention. "Not many people would see that. You've got a wee bit close. Can we change the subject?"

"Sure, sorry, wasn't my intention."

"So as we're here for our children," Lizzie smiled and raised her mug of tea, "What does Sam see in Rowan that makes him so happy?"

Strains of acoustic guitar and singing filled the air above them.

"He knows she fancies him but she behaves as if she wants to be friends."

Lizzie hung her head. "Go on."

"I don't know any of this, by the way. It's only what I think."

"Go on."

"He likes the fact she's smart, isn't too hung up on make-up and fashion but more than that. He likes that she thinks for herself. You, okay?"

She was weary. Weary but happy. Lizzie nodded. "I'm good and thank you. You've given me my first indication that I might be doing an okay job as a parent."

Lizzie lay awake staring at her bedroom ceiling, the flaking cracks and the paper lampshade. She wasn't a real witch. A real witch would be in her circle, performing her full moon ritual. A real witch didn't succumb to confusion and exhaustion after three latish nights and a single bottle of wine. A real witch fought the frailties of the human form, for the benefit of the higher self. Lizzie huddled beneath the covers.

She dreamed of Richard. He stood on a hilltop, the Sorcerer's Apprentice, summoning spoons to make more jam until she was washed away on a sweet pink river. A convergence ahead made her choose and though she paddled hard and furiously against the current, she was whisked away from Matt's arms as he waited for her in the other channel. Through a tunnel, the jam flowed on and Lizzie emerged in a world full of exotically scented flowers displaying petals of stunning brilliance against a cerulean sky. The people were swathed in colour too or they wore bright shoes or carried luminous handbags. Marsha was

49

there, gold jewellery dripping from her neck and ears and cascading down her crinkled brown arms. Josh and Bryony each held one of Rowan's hands, swinging her like a three year old between them. Her laughter mingled with the call of the gulls as the river widened out before joining with the sea. The beach was decked with shimmering umbrellas, their centres black so from above, as Lizzie soared with the gulls, a field of glossy poppies bobbed beneath her. Everyone was smiling. Until a pair of giant marauding stilettos sent the people scurrying and screaming.

7

She wore her latest charity shop find, a sleeveless loose fitting tent of whites, lilacs and blues which she pulled in with a ribbon below her bust. With her auburn curls twisted into a knot on her head and confined behind a green and lilac scarf, she was as anxious as Marianne Dashwood, before her first ball. Louise greeted her with a wolf whistle.

"You look stunning! Good weekend?"

"Yes, and you?"

"Really good, thanks. Terry's team are through to the knockout rounds. You must come."

"Let's get today over with, shall we?"

"Sorry, you're right but I know you'll be fine."

"Thanks, Lou."

Work arriving on her desk had changed. There were still the usual legal documents, agendas and emails but personnel work was the greater load, especially the handwritten notes from Edward, David and Tom after the interviews of the current staff. Lizzie struggled to type the words but not read them. The lives of her work colleagues were being decided by her bosses at their whim and fancy, or so it seemed to her, but she couldn't speak of it or do anything about it. She recited nursery rhymes in her head, to keep the meanings from her mind. A dry mouth and a head ache forced her to call Suzanne.

Lizzie splashed her face in the basin of the ladies room before dabbing it with a paper towel to dry. She heard the stifled sobs in the cubicle. Tania's shoes.

"You okay, Tania?"

Tania blew her nose and emerged. Her blue-grey eyes were ringed with pink and her nose glowed. "It's all this…waiting! Sorry, I'm so sensitive today."

"I've been like it all weekend. Luckily, the weather allowed me to get outside and keep busy or I would have burst. You sure you're okay? I'm making tea."

Tania shook her head before turning to the mirror. "I'll clean up and get on. Won't be long to wait now."

The message flashed onto Lizzie's computer screen. She was to be outside Edward Brown's office at ten minutes to three precisely. It had been David's office but he now occupied the old archive store, while the files were confined to the basement. Lizzie's mind was racing. Why did David let his uncle walk all over him? He and Tom have been making profits for the company for years. Would she lose her job if she were a minute early or a minute late?

Peter Lucas strolled through the Edward Brown's office door, carrying a folder and smirking. He nodded at Lizzie as he made his way to the main office. Suzanne was acting as Edward's secretary. Edward had already returned two temps for not meeting his exacting standards. Suzanne caught Lizzie's eye. The buzz on Suzanne's desk made them both jump.

"You can go in now."

Edward Brown sat behind his desk. David hovered by the window. Tom was absent, as was Chantelle from HR. Lizzie looked at David who tried to smile, creasing his face into a contorted death mask. She looked away.

"Mrs Martin, your re-interview confirms you have the qualifications and skills for your job."

Lizzie sighed. "Thank you."

"But your appearance is, shall we say, somewhat Bohemian. This is an office, not a garden party. Smarten up and you keep your job. This is your new contract. If you agree, sign it. That'll be all."

"Sorry?"

"Your job's safe, Lizzie." David stepped to her side. "You only need to tone down the outfits a little." He raised her from her seat and she pushed back her chair, shaking his arm from hers.

"A little! A lot, my girl!" Edward Brown stood, black eyes glistening beneath his brows in a bright red face. "No more of this billowing drapery! I want our corporate image reflected the moment a client arrives at our door and that means skirt, blouse, jacket and heels on reception! "

"But…"

Edward Brown glared and Lizzie allowed herself to be guided from the room by David.

Why had she agreed to this? Because she needed company. Days of worrying about her job could do that to a person but why had she thought for a moment Matt would understand?

"It's only a suit."

"But it's the principle and there is no dress code in the contract."

"Your contract's only probationary. Did you read the new one they gave you?"

Lizzie shook her head.

"If this boss man is as strict as you say, I reckon it'll be in the contract."

"But why is it so important to him? You're an artist. You should understand my point of view! It's about personal freedom, to be the person you are!"

"Whoa! I'm not making you do it." He lowered his voice as other drinkers stared at them. They sat on a bench at the far end of the pub balcony, catching the last rays of light from the setting sun.

"I know but…"

"It's the equivalent of school uniform, Liz. Think of it like that. It's a requirement. Accept it. I thought we were celebrating."

"What?"

"You told me on the phone your job was safe."

There it was again. Impatience.

"But at what cost?"

"Let it go."

And she did, right there, in front of strangers, in the face of someone she barely knew.

"You bloody hypocrite! You were the one who wanted me to stand up to my boss!"

"No I didn't. Look, I'm telling you to view it as a small price to pay…"

"Stop telling me what to do! You don't know me or anything about me because you haven't bothered to try to find out! You've been far too busy looking down my top and trying to look at my legs through my skirt! Ten days I've been kept waiting to find out if I can keep my own bloody job and all the while, these men have known I'm capable but want to show their control over me, by making me worry and now, by dictating what I should wear and you think they have the right to do that!"

She climbed out of the bench seat and pointed in Matt's face. "No man is going to tell me what to wear!"

Lizzie walked unsteadily along the balcony to applause and cheers from the women drinkers. She hung tightly to the banister rail as she descended, her outburst having weakened her knees and her confidence. She was in the country somewhere between Brentwood and Hutton. She would have to call a taxi.

"Lizzie!"

She turned to the voice. She recognised the face. Her head spun with disbelief and anguish before she fainted.

8

Furious hornets fought in her ears and her eyes refused to open. A rumble of voices penetrated her skull. A single female gentle tone pierced the chaos.

"Lie still, you're okay. I've got your hand."

Lizzie opened her eyes. A kindly female face peered at her with concern. The owner of the face held her hand, gently stroking it. Lizzie winced at the humanity staring down on her and tried to get up.

"Ooooh!" She clasped her head.

"Lay still, love. You hit your head on the table on the way down. Ambulance is on its way."

"I...where am I? Oh, the pub...Ooooh!" A zap of pain shut her eyes. Shivers traced over her skin, a million tiny spiders ready to bite.

"Stay with me, love. What's your name? Where's that blanket? She's going into shock!"

A squeeze of her hand brought her back. "Liz, Liz McCartney, Martin. Rowan!"

"I can call someone for you, love but you have to stay with me."

Soft wool caressed her skin. She was floating on a fluffy cloud. It was peaceful here.

"Who's Martin, Liz? Who's Rowan?"

Lizzie's eyes flashed open. "My daughter. No! Call my friend. Call Louise."

It wasn't a smell as such, more an absence of any that stirred Lizzie and she opened her eyes to a stark white room. Monitors beeped and whirred and tubes and lines violated her body. Her scream brought nurses running.

With the oxygen mask off her face, Lizzie kept apologising.

"Don't you worry, Mrs Martin. You've had a rough few days…"

"Days!" Lizzie tried to sit up. Gentle but strong arms restrained her.

"Now, none of that. I need to run a few tests and take some blood. If I'm happy, we'll see about getting you a cup of tea."

Tears erupted from Lizzie's eyes. "But my daughter, please. Is Rowan okay?"

"Dark hair, stunning brown eyes?"

Lizzie tried to smile but more tears fell.

"She's fine." Nurse Mycroft lifted the clip board from the foot of Lizzie's bed and flipped a few pages. "Mrs Davies, Louise Davies, was contacted at the scene and she came here before she and her husband fetched Rowan from home. They've been here with your daughter in the evenings and most of the weekend. Mrs Davies' husband drove Rowan to school today, I believe."

Sobs engulfed Lizzie. Nurse Mycroft handed her tissues. Lizzie struggled as the wires and tubes constricted her movement.

"Go gently now."

Nurse Mycroft's round face softened and she patted Lizzie's arm. "She's a lovely girl, your daughter and a sensible one, if I may say. She was upset, of course, but Mrs Davies assured her you would wake when your body was ready. She was right."

"And it's Monday?"

Nurse Mycroft nodded. "Tests, then we'll see about tea." A buzzer bleeped at her belt. She glanced at the digital box. "I have to run. You rest and I'll send Phoebe in. No more talking, you hear?"

Lizzie tried to nod then wished she hadn't. The bandages around her head were tight. Her scalp burned and the canon ball in her head swelled. She shut her eyes and tried to remember what had happened to cause her to be in hospital with a head containing a molten anvil.

She sat on the grass on the river bank and watched him. The man swayed like a reed in the breeze, the half empty bottle in his hand. The sun was setting in a grey sky, the orange glow staining the ominous rain clouds with rust. He staggered towards the bridge. Lizzie watched his penultimate act, bending to place the rock on the paper. He straightened up and lumbered on.

In the centre of the bridge, the man paused. The amber liquid drained into his mouth. He leaned against the rail. The empty bottle somersaulted in the air and she watched the man follow it.

Sweat prickled her face and chest. A whimper escaped.

"I'm here, Mum."

The dream was over and this was real. Rowan was here! Rowan was fine! Lizzie opened her eyes and quickly closed them as pain squirted venom into her eyes. She heard the curtains being drawn and fluttered her eyelids open.

"Rowan, I'm so sorry."

"What for, Mum? You didn't get pissed and make a fool of yourself, or anything. You slipped in the bar and fell and hit your head. It was an accident."

Lizzie tried to smile. She looked behind Rowan and Louise's worried face appeared. "Lou."

"I'm here and Rowan's fine and you will be soon." She sat on the edge of the bed.

"Tell me what they said happened…when they called and after."

"Don't you remember?"

"No, I've been trying. I went to work in my Jane Austen dress and they told me…work! I haven't contacted…"

"All done and dusted. Don't you worry. I emailed Tom Melchett on Wednesday night. He's always seemed more down to earth than David, odd those Brown's…anyway, Tom called me almost immediately and asked if there was anything he could do."

Tears flushed Lizzie's cheeks. "I've let them down and you, Rowan."

"Stop, Mum, you haven't."

Louise took the tissue box and dried Lizzie's face. She gave her the box and Lizzie could reach for it. She was only attached to one machine.

"What's done is done, you know that. If you've finished blubbing, I've been told you can have a tea."

"I'll get it." Rowan squeezed Lizzie's arm, unleashing another flood, and shaking her head, left the room.

Lizzie stemmed the flow of tears and blew her nose with clumsy hands. "Tell me, Lou about Wednesday night."

"The landlady called to say you'd slipped in the Thatcher's Arms and hit your head. The ambulance had arrived and they were taking you to Queen's. I said I'd meet them there."

"But why was I there? Why did I fall in the bar?"

Louise shook her head. "You weren't drunk, they told me that. Rowan said you were out with a friend. I did my best on your admission form but thought Rowan would do better and she needed to know so I phoned Terry. His mate dropped him over and he came with me to collect Rowan. I didn't know if she'd need me and I couldn't do that if I was driving but she's a good girl. You've done a brilliant job bringing her up, love."

"Thanks, thanks for everything. And Terry too."

"He doesn't mind. He's a good one, one of the best."

"Lucky you, lucky both of you. What happened to me when they brought me in? My head hurts like hell."

"Honestly?"

"Yes."

"You were covered in blood from your head wound and your heart beat was erratic. That's all I know. They had worked on you when I came back with Rowan, cleaned you up a lot and you were going off for a head scan, I think."

"So is this ICU?"

Louise nodded. "But you won't stay here long now. They'll want to get you on a ward as soon as there's a bed."

Nurse Mycroft, preceded by Rowan with a tray of teas, continued the conversation. "If your tea stays down and you feel hungry, you can have a biscuit but take it slowly. You've a drip still in and I'll do your blood pressure now. Keep calm and still and you'll be on a ward by tomorrow."

The cuff tightened on Lizzie's arm. "Can you tell me, what did I do, to my head?"

"You knocked yourself out cold on a wooden table. Gash is about four inches but it's all stitched up. Itchy?"

"Sore."

"It'll itch soon but sore and itchy mean it's healing. Let me know though, if you feel unwell or there's a change with your head."

"It feels like a bowling ball is trying to escape."

"That's everything settling down. Sleep is your friend. Sleep often. You should wake each time feeling a little better. This is fine." She unwrapped the cuff. "Not much longer, ladies. Enjoy your tea then call it a night."

Lizzie struggled to bring the cup to her mouth so Rowan helped her. Sublime hot liquid trickled down her throat. She relaxed back. Tears flowed. "It's the helplessness. Sorry."

"Well, talking of bowling, it's coming up for eight o'clock and I'm due to pick Terry up at nine. If we go now, Rowan, we can fit a game in, if you fancy it?"

"Yeah, great, thanks Lou. Mum, I rang Nanny Martin and Granny McCartney but Dad's phone goes straight to answerphone. I left a message. I thought he should know. Nana sends her love and said something about a shark, couldn't really make it out. Granny...sends her love. She said she will visit you when you're home."

"Thanks, Rowan. You've done a great job. Don't worry about Granny. She doesn't do blood or hospitals. What about homework?"

Rowan turned to Louise. "Told you she was better."

9

She woke to the smell of faeces. The ward bustled with staff dressed in navy, pale blue and green. The stench drifted over from a curtained bed.

"That's dis-gust-ing!" The young girl in the bed on Lizzie's left, pronounced all three syllables with venom. "Some of us are trying to eat breakfast over here!"

"It's under control, Lucy. Keep your voice down." A weary-faced nurse hurried to Lizzie's bedside. "What did you want for breakfast, Elizabeth?"

"Lizzie, um, I don't know, do you have cereal?"

"Take your pick." The nurse gestured to the trolley. "Juice?"

"Yes, please and cornflakes."

The items were placed on the table over her bed. "Trolley will be along in a bit with hot drinks." The nurse picked up Lizzie's clipboard. "Take it slow with the eating. Just a little for now. We can always find you a banana if you're peckish again before lunch."

"Thanks."

A sweet, sickly disinfectant aroma replaced the odour of the farmyard. Staff departed but the cubicle remained curtained.

"Nurse! What about me?" The elderly woman opposite Lizzie waved her concern.

"You're okay, Elsie, you've got your breakfast on your table. Have a look."

Elsie looked down, surprise and then pleasure evident on her face.

"Bless her." The nurse trundled out of the ward.

"So what you in for?"

"I hit my head."

"Well, I can see that, you div. You look like you've escaped from a tomb!"

"Why ask then?"

"Oooo! Hark at you! I was being friendly."

Lizzie turned to Lucy. Her head screamed. She wanted to be nice. She was always kind and patient. "You were being nosy, not nice. Leave me alone."

"Don't worry, I will!"

Lizzie spooned a teaspoon of cereal into her mouth and tried to chew. Her ears buzzed and nausea twisted in her stomach. She sipped her juice and the pain subsided.

A gentle voice from Lizzie's right calmed her. "I expect it's the injury, why you're feeling less charitable this morning, dear. Pain can make you do all sorts of things. I'm Brenda. In for my second new hip and looking forward to getting out of here, like everyone else. No need to turn, I can see it's painful for you."

"Hello, Brenda. Sorry, Lucy. My head's not my own today."

"You're alright, Lizzie. I was being nosy. When you're in this dump every month, other people's lives are appealing."

"Nurse, nurse!"

64

"Elsie, your breakfast's on your table."

"Nurse, nurse!"

Lucy, broad, blond and buxom, pushed a walking frame into view as she approached Elsie's bed. "Here you go, Elsie."

Once again, surprise registered on Elsie's face. She dipped her knife in the marmalade pot and smeared it on her bread. "Where's my tea?"

"They'll be round in a bit. Anyone need anything while I'm up?"

"I'll have a newspaper."

"Me too, thanks Lucy."

Lizzie let her head fall back on the pillows and shut her eyes as a strange new world played out its day. It wasn't the pain making her snap. She was naked. Naked, injured and helpless and surrounded by strangers. Her faded yellow nightgown belonged to the hospital. Her hair was covered in a shroud. Anonymous, naked and scared, Lizzie longed for her Sanctuary. Hot drinks arrived closely followed by a trolley dripping with sweets and magazines. She heard their voices but she drifted away, taking her heavy head with her.

Lizzie woke to a sandwich, banana and juice on her tray and a hunched figure reading a book by her bedside. She reached for a tissue and knocked the juice over.

"Let me."

Richard Parker mopped up the spillage, managing to save half the contents of the carton. "Can I help you with this?"

"I'll be okay." Lizzie gulped the rest of the orange juice. Richard watched. She was in a nightgown in front of Sam's father and definitely not looking her best. The empty carton fell from her fingers. "I can't seem to focus on anything. Thanks and thanks for coming."

"Sam told me Thursday morning. Rowan rang him late Wednesday night. She wanted to let him know she was staying with friends. Your friend from work?"

"Louise works security for my building. She's been amazing."

"You helped with her stall, at the Charity Fayre?"

Lizzie nodded.

"Sam said Rowan's happy to stay with her. Seems they have a full satellite package. I think they're arranging a movie night."

Lizzie's mouth attempted a smile.

"So, how're you feeling?"

"A lot better but my head doesn't feel it belongs to me. And I'm tired. Very very tired."

"I'll go." Richard went to get up.

"No, stay. If you don't mind. It's good to see a familiar face." The face of a grey haired man with vibrant green eyes flashed into her mind and was gone.

"Sam said you fell. In a bar."

"Seems so. I don't remember anything. Not going there or who I was with or anything. It's so frustrating. Days of my life have disappeared. And today's Tuesday?"

Richard nodded. "Were you drinking? Look, I only mean…well, how did your interview go? Was that why you were out?"

"I don't know. Talk to me. Tell me about your weekend, or something. I want to hear normal."

Richard smiled and sat on the bed beside her. His cheeks were flushed in the sealed hospital ward and he took a swig from a water bottle.

"Before six, I was out in the garden, drinking coffee and reading. Had breakfast with Sam about eleven, scrambled eggs and bacon and then we had a swim. In fact, we were in and out of the pool most of the day."

"You have a pool?"

She watched the blush rise in Richard's face. "Came with the house. As did the hot tub. Is it overly pretentious?"

"No, I was thinking Rowan would love it. She's always been a water baby and I've tried to encourage her."

"When you're out of here, you must both come over. We'll make a day of it. Have a barbeque, if you fancy."

Lizzie allowed his warm, caring energy to wash over her. Home. She wanted to be home. She needed her Sanctuary, her space, her goddess. She reached for Richard's hand. "Go on."

"We didn't do much else Saturday. We had takeaway Chinese in the evening. Sam's drummer came round and they hung out by the pool. Sunday, I jogged before six and did the house clean. I took Sam to practise."

"Mrs Martin?"

A nurse in a navy blue uniform attempted to restrain the man behind her from approaching the bed. "Mrs Martin, do you know this man?"

Despite her head pounding like a coin stamp on speed, Lizzie smiled. Two men sat by her bedside, unfurling their feathers and strutting their intentions. It made her dizzy, two men claiming her as their concern but she enjoyed watching them, and the more they talked, the more she remembered.

"So now you've introduced yourselves, I was in the pub with you, Matt. What happened?"

"Don't you remember? You were upset and went to the ladies. I went to find you and you'd gone."

"You're lying," said Richard.

"Who are you calling a liar? Does this man have to stay? He's only the father of a friend of your daughter."

"Richard stays. Why was I upset?"

"About your job. You…"

"I argued with you. Something about my job and then I went to leave…didn't you hear the noise in the bar?"

"I went straight outside."

"You said you went to find Lizzie."

"Butt out! This has nothing to do with you! I did go to find you. Outside."

"You didn't hear anything? Wonder about the commotion in the bar?"

"I told you to stay out of this!" Matt took Lizzie's hand. "We can't talk properly while he's here."

Lizzie extricated her hand. Matt's face wore a blond fluffy beard. Hair frizzed around his face and his pony tail was lank and greasy. In the confines of the ward, he smelled sour.

"When did you leave?"

"When I couldn't find you."

"But you didn't call until Sunday."

"I…no, I called Thursday. Thursday morning to see if you were alright."

"Rowan gave me my phone. You didn't call until Sunday. The ambulance arrived at the pub and you left me."

"No!" Matt stood up. "I took you out to celebrate. Your job was safe but there were conditions. You were upset and disappeared, I told you."

"And you didn't think to go into the bar?"

"You!" Matt pointed an angry finger. "The ladies room isn't in the bar!"

"You said you went outside." Richard stood up. "Do I know you? Your face seems familiar. Have we met before?"

"Not likely! Look, I have to go, Lizzie. Call me when you get out and we'll arrange to get together."

Lizzie scanned the men's faces, one angry and impatient, the other thoughtful and pensive.

"Okay."

Matt leaned in to kiss her. She couldn't move her head in time. His lips tasted of whisky and soot. He hurried from the ward without a backward glance.

"Do you really know him?"

Richard shrugged. "I've looked at a lot of mug shots in my time."

"Matt can't be a criminal! He's a credit controller and sings in a band. Don't look at me like that. He's not endearing himself to me at the moment either."

"Like mother, like daughter." Richard grinned.

"Only she's far better taste than me! I remember why we argued, me and Matt. I won't be calling him, don't worry."

Richard raised both hands in surrender. "Not my business."

"No but you're right. We've only been for a few walks and a meal, that's all and I'm glad. Rowan's Dad was…let's say unpredictable and our relationship somewhat volatile. I don't need that again, ever."

A trolley bounced into the ward, rattling cups and jugs. Lizzie drank tea with Richard.

"If you remember, where you've seen Matt, you will tell me."

"Like I said, I've seen a lot of faces. I know you want to fill in the blanks, the parts you don't remember but if I were you, I'd rest up and get out of here first."

"You're right. Do you mind if I sleep?"

"You go for it. You look a lot better than when you first woke, by the way."

"Thanks. I haven't dared ask for a mirror."

"Ah, well be prepared for your face to look tired, Liz."

"That bad?"

"You're bound to be tired."

Tears flowed freely and Richard gave her the tissue box. "Sorry."

"No need."

"I'm so shallow."

His gentle words moved her. "No you're not, Liz. You've been through a major trauma."

He held her hand as she sobbed. "And all I can think about is whether I've got any hair left."

10

Richard, Sam and Rowan collected her from hospital the following Monday afternoon. She had tried to push the discharge through for Friday but paperwork couldn't be signed off and completed until after the weekend. Feeling better, Lizzie had spent her time with a notebook, writing down all she remembered and with a sketchbook, drawing faces. Nurses, patients and visitors were committed to paper, their profiles and eccentricities flowing through Lizzie's pencil. She dozed through most of Saturday, between sketches, so lay awake all night, watching the minutes tick by on the clock above the door. On Sunday, Rowan pushed her from the ward and they shared tea and flapjack in the cafeteria, before Lizzie insisted on being pushed through the doors to the sunshine outside. A cool breeze chilled her skin until Rowan pushed her round the corner and the healing warmth of the sun bestowed blessings on her body.

Louise met them at the house, which was spotless and gleaming. Even her bedroom didn't look too bad. Louise made her comfortable in bed for a sleep.

"Thanks so much for this, Lou. I know I need to decorate this room, but I did Rowan's and the lounge…"

"Enough. Get some rest."

"But it's so shabby."

Louise brushed back her ebony fringe, stuck to her face by the warm weather. "It doesn't matter, Liz. No one's judging you. Get some rest. The more you sleep, the better you'll feel."

By Saturday, with Louise's help, Lizzie was on her feet again. She added the final items to her trug. The kettle gave up its last drop of water to her flask and she opened the back door. The front door bell rang.

"Mum! What a lovely surprise."

Beneath the faded sun shade, they sat with a tray of tea between them.

"Cake looks lovely."

"You obviously need it. You look like something out of Belsen. I told you being a vegetablarian would make you ill. I should have brought steak, not cake!"

"I'm always well, Mum but I was in the ICU for almost a week and unconscious for half of that, after the accident."

Mrs McCartney lifted her nose as if a bad smell was beneath it. "Accident?"

"Yes, I slipped somehow and hit my head."

"But you were in a bar, Elizabeth. You'd obviously been drinking. What can you expect?" She wafted away a fly before picking up her tea cup.

"I wasn't drunk."

Disappointment washed over Lizzie like an icy shower. Conversations with her mother were always the same, her mother accusing and Lizzie needing to defend herself about deeds she hadn't done and words she hadn't spoken.

She'd hoped her mother would soften, maybe understand a need for compromise so the women could enjoy a happier relationship.

"Well, you would say that!"

Mrs McCartney blew an insect from her crisp white blouse, wrinkling her nose as more flies buzzed around the tea tray. Lizzie cut them cake and handed a plate to her mother. "Oh, you don't own cake forks do you?"

"No, there's kitchen roll for your fingers."

They ate in silence, the sun beaming down on them and the dry grass sizzling in the heat.

"Delicious, Mum. Thanks."

"Where's Rowan?"

"At a friend's house. She's working on her art project for September."

Mrs McCartney raised her eyebrows into her blue rinsed curls. "You're not encouraging her to draw are you? She's got a brain, Elizabeth! She should be studying physics and chemistry and maths."

"Rowan's taking art, history and biology for her options, as well as physics, chemistry and maths."

"I could have been a doctor, you know. I was always an 'A' grade student…"

Mrs McCartney talked. Lizzie had heard it all before, her grand parents' lack of funds, the inconvenience of her granddad's ill health and her mother's martyrdom, giving up on her first choice of career and taking a job to help support them.

"My sister, your Aunt Eleanor was useless!"

"Why did you come?"

74

"I beg your pardon?"

"Why did you come here today? I almost died in hospital, I'm sitting here with a bandage on my head like the mummy from the crypt and you've done nothing but reprimand me for my lifestyle choices and my parenting skills!" Wow! Did I say that? Perhaps a blow on the head's done me good.

"Well, really! I've made the journey…

"In a cab."

"I've made the journey, all this way, to come and visit my daughter and that's the thanks I get!" Mrs McCartney dabbed her lips with her paper towel, scrunched it and threw it on her plate.

"Dad would've asked me how I was, how Rowan was, be sad he missed her and offer to make the tea."

"I didn't come here to talk about your father." Mrs McCartney stood up.

"Sit down, Mum, please. I think we should."

Mrs McCartney sat. "Your father was a fool, Elizabeth."

"That's not how I remember him."

"Of course you don't! You were so alike!"

"And that's why we fight."

"We do not fight! All families have disagreements."

"But you disagree with everything I do. When I've needed support, all you've done is knock me lower."

"You make your bed, you lie in it!"

Lizzie gasped. "How can you say that?"

Mrs McCartney hung her head. She snapped it up and her piercing stare scared Lizzie. "I saved you from your father."

"Leave. Go. I've nothing to say to you."

"You'd turn your own mother out?"

"No, I'll call you a cab."

Lizzie leaned on the door jamb. The tail lights of the cab disappeared down the road as a black car drew up and Sam and Rowan climbed out. Richard waved from the car.

"Hey, Mum, was that Granny?"

Lizzie bit her lip and nodded.

"Rowan, best I don't come in. Maybe dinner another time."

Lizzie tried to smile. Sam's sensitivity warmed her. He could see she was upset. "You're welcome, Sam. Does your Dad want to stay? It'll be a bit various."

"Aren't all your meals, Mum?"

She was glad they stayed for dinner. The children lifted her mood and she always felt relaxed in Richard's company. Did she fancy him? He was fanciable, no doubt about that but he'd built a wall, a wall of protection not dissimilar to her armour. Friendship was what he offered and she welcomed it with open arms. This evening, she caught him staring at her. She'd blushed, as had he and longed to ask him what he was thinking. They left before ten with an arrangement made for a bowling evening.

The Sanctuary welcomed her. It had been her refuge most days since leaving hospital. Painting was part of her life again but not tonight.

With her old oak wand, she cast her circle and within its protective wall, she grew her forest. Ancient trunks soared into the blue, vast canopies of leaves shielding the forest floor beneath. Lizzie's feet traced a worn track between the columns until the old wood was replaced by bright new saplings of oak, ash, birch, beech and rowan. She smelled the vibrant green of new life and abundance and walked on towards the glade.

With her red bunches tickling her shoulders and her fawn sandals scuffing up the twigs, little Lizzie rushed into the opening of trees and into the arms of her father. There was no course stubble on his chin or stinking breath on her cheek. Her father was auburn, bonny and clear skinned and his eyes shone, the emerald eyes of the fae.

"What happened to us, Dad?"

"Oh, Lizzie, I never stopped loving you."

"You abandoned me, to her! You were always away and when you came back, you didn't want to hug me anymore!"

"Oh, Lizzie, my little flower. I did what was best."

"You didn't love me anymore! You didn't want to see my paintings!"

The beauty of the fae fell from her father and she held him as he sobbed into her shoulder. She left the Lizzie child in the forest. She was a woman now but none the wiser.

Almost a week later, Lizzie sat at Louise's kitchen table with a plastic gown around her shoulders. The hospital had done their best but if she was going back to work, she needed her hair cut properly. Louise's friend Jane stood ready with the scissors.

"What do you think, Janey?"

"Depends how much length you wanted to keep. Most of this is matted with blood. I can keep some at the top to cover the scar."

Louise placed her hand on Lizzie's shoulder. "What do you think?"

Lizzie cuffed at her eyes. "Why is hair so important? I miss it not hanging over me, you know. I guess we have to cut the bad stuff out. It won't wash."

"It'll grow back." She patted Lizzie's shoulder and nodded to Jane.

In under an hour, the thin grey face in the mirror wore a shock of red curls around her head like hennaed dandelion fluff.

Lizzie lay on her side but sleep refused to come. She had wept for the loss of her hair, grieving for the woman who had grown it as part of her armour. Naked and lonely, wrapped in a blanket, she made her way to the bottom of the garden.

Her desk was littered with sketches and pinned on a string were three faces captured in watercolour. Louise's kindness shone from her image, her black hair highlighted with blue like a raven's wing while Rowan's face flickered from girl to woman, depending how you looked at it. Sam's face shone from the paper, mischievous blue eyes ready to wink.

There were landscapes, verdant green valleys looked over by towering grey mountains and a meadow with a pond and a vibrant dragonfly in the foreground.

Abandoning her wrap and inspired by the images on her desk, Lizzie cast her circle, her favourite standing stones protecting her as she worked. She called in the elements, each welcomed and thanked for their presence and she called in the God of the Forest, Cernunnos, to take part in her ritual. All was ready within the Sanctuary. She felt the pulse of the ancient rock, blue stone, limestone and granite. She heard the energy rising and bursting from the trees she loved so much. She had force in abundance. Calling in the goddess would create the perfect balance.

Facing north, with a wooden carved owl in her hand, Lizzie called in Cerridwen.

> *"Cerridwen, storyteller, seeker and weaver*
> *I call you to my aid*
> *Blessed Mother, Goddess of inspiration and transformation*
> *Hear my prayer."*

Cross legged on the floor in front of her rusty cauldron, Lizzie shut her eyes.

> *"Goddess Cerridwen, wise woman of the land*
> *Allow me to see so I may understand."*

Lizzie opened her eyes. The water in the cauldron gleamed oily black and moved, spinning into a spiral before settling on an image of a family living room. The gas fire blazed, the retro green curtains were drawn. Her parents were arguing. Lizzie listened, the voice of Cerridwen warning her.

> *"My cauldron shows you what has been*
> *Now once bidden, never unseen."*

11

Lizzie was welcomed at work as the returning conqueror. Her head of new curls was admired and her determination to get back to work, applauded. By the main office. She hadn't taken a sip of coffee at her desk before the phone rang and she was summoned to Edward Brown's office.

"You're back to normal?"

"I think so. I may need to take a few more breaks away from my screen than I used to but I'll save up my printing and copying for when my head starts to ache."

"Or make up the time at the end of the day."

"It won't come to that."

She stood bravely in a plain olive green maxi dress, tied at the waist with a matching plaited cord and with another plait twisted in her hair, asserting her intentions with all the confidence she could muster. Tom had made sure she received full pay while she was off, a kind gesture as she was still on probation, so she wanted to prove his faith in her was justified.

"Not much improvement with your clothes, Mrs Martin."

"It's only one colour."

"But I can't see your legs, woman! It's another sack. And no heels."

"I'll have to learn, you see, to wear heels and because of my head injury…"

"Yes, yes, I know. You'll get vertigo and burst a blood vessel or something. Seems to be any excuse!"

"I was only going to say that my balance hasn't been as good since, well, the accident and I didn't want to fall off my heels in reception while meeting a client. That wouldn't be professional, would it?" Don't smile. Look serious. Nearly over.

"No, no, very well but you understand this can't go on. You've got six weeks to conform and sign your contract."

"Thanks for this, Lou. I've done three days and I'm shattered."

Louise sipped from her wine glass. "How's the head?"

"Muzzy all the time, hurts a bit sometimes but as long as I don't look at the screen all day, I think I can cope. I brought my sketch book in so if I've run out of printing or copying, I can draw."

"I wish I could! Never been able to draw a straight line, me! Terry's arty. He used to work shifts and be back by four in the afternoon. He took up pottery, got quite good at it. We've all the gear in a shed in the garden."

"Really?"

"Trouble is, with his new job, he's later home and then there's the bowling."

Lizzie nodded. "I've enjoyed having time to paint but now I'm back at work…"

"You paint too? You clever, kitty. What do you paint with?"

"Colour?"

"You know what I mean."

"I used to…well, in the past…look, I'm getting back into it, okay? I'm using watercolour at the moment."

Louise held up her hands. "Okay, okay, I only asked!"

"Sorry, sorry, my painting…I'm a bit, well, sensitive about it but honestly, it's not only that. I saw my mother last week and I have to see her again."

"You didn't say."

"I needed time to think. We argued, properly because I didn't let her trample all over me."

"Is that good or bad?"

Lizzie sighed. "Bad we argued because I told her to go and put her in a cab but I suppose it's good that I stood up to her for once."

"Of course it's good! She needs to show you some respect!"

"The same day, Rowan came home and brought Sam and Richard stayed and I was beginning to relax when the phone rang. Rowan brought me the message. My mother informed her to tell me that she didn't like bad feeling so if I apologised properly, she would forget the incident and everything could go back to the way it was."

"And you obviously won't apologise."

"No."

"And you've had all this malarkey going down while trying to get ready to get back to work? No wonder your head hurts!"

"I know but, surprisingly, I've coped with it well."

"Not so surprising if you've been painting."

Lizzie stared at Louise, her mouth beginning to scowl.

"I only meant Terry used to say he did his thinking with clay in his hands and he could put his feelings into it, as you do with paint. Oh, Liz."

Louise shuffled closer on the bench seat and Lizzie cried into her shoulder. She quickly extricated herself and blew her nose.

"You know how I tick. You're so clever, Lou."

"Am I?"

Lizzie smiled, sniffed and rubbed her forehead.

"Ouchy?"

"Yes, I need to get home." She drained the last of her lime and water. "Lou, I found out something. Something about my past and I'm going to confront my Mum about it. Wise?"

"Depends. You need to follow through the consequences."

"What do you mean?"

"You said you found something out. You going to tell me what or how?"

Lizzie shook her head.

"Okay, fair enough. Let's say you ask your Mum if something is true, be prepared for both answers."

Lizzie hugged her friend. "I said you were clever."

The sunshine bubble had burst and warm summer rain descended. The bowling alley was seething with noisy, sweaty bodies. Lizzie sighed. Her festival trousers were already sticking to her legs and her head was full of lead. She accepted a lime and water once seated in their lane and watched Sam showing Rowan how to bowl. Her

84

hands were bigger than Lizzie's with long graceful fingers. With her first ball, she knocked down six skittles and cleared the rest with her second to cheers from the other three.

She flopped down beside Lizzie. "This is awesome! I had one game with Lou but haven't let on to Sam. He seems keen to tutor me in the art of bowling."

She was about to lecture her daughter about the dangers of playing those kinds of games when her turn was called and she shuffled forward, head bent and grumbling. Richard searched for a ball on their rig before pushing through the crowds and returning triumphant with an orange ball. It fitted her fingers well but because of that, it was light and her first attempt landed in the gulley. Her second took one skittle before following the first.

"We need to find you a weightier ball but with small finger holes." Richard stood scanning the rig to his left.

"We really don't."

"That one might do."

She watched Sam or rather, she watched Rowan watching Sam. His strike received a high five and a shoulder nudge in return but it was the eyes worrying Lizzie.

Rowan took aim and sent all the skittles flying. And then she did it again. Lizzie prayed Sam's admiring looks were only for Rowan's bowling prowess.

"Here you go."

Lizzie took the black ball, weightier but with the required finger holes. She took aim and sent all the skittles back to where they came from.

85

"Thanks for this Richard, but we could have gone back to ours for food."

"My treat, the whole evening. I've enjoyed it. Got to team up with my son, even though we lost to you ladies."

Rowan waved her pizza at Lizzie. "You were cool, Mum. Can we come again, please?"

"As a treat, why not!"

"Can I have my birthday here? Jess and Emma would love it!"

"I…don't know. We'll see." Lizzie took a bite of pizza and pushed salad around her bowl.

"When's your birthday?" asked Sam.

"Not 'til October so Mum can save up."

"I said we'll see. You might change your mind and want something else by then." How I hate this subterfuge about money!

"Mine and Dad's are in December," persisted Sam.

"Two Sagittarians, a Cancerian and a Scorpion. No wonder we get on so well, though your moon sign and other alignments have more bearing on overall personality. What?" said Rowan, shrugging at Lizzie's wide-eyed stare.

"I didn't know you were into astrology."

"I'm not but I love the ancient Egyptians and they were. Lots of tribes were."

Rowan talked while the others listened, food forgotten.

"The monuments they built were aligned to the stars and planets. That's astronomy not astrology but I picked up a few bits of that along the way. And it's not only the Egyptians! Neolithic and stone age man weren't grunting savages! They built huge complicated earth works and monuments and transported...do you know, Mum?"

"What, darling?"

"I really wish I didn't have to do these next two years at school."

Lizzie struggled to hide her astonishment at Rowan's passionate outburst. "Why's that?"

"I love art and history, classics and drama, you know that, but I want to study archaeology and anthropology and find out more about our ancestors."

About to leave the front of the car, Lizzie changed her mind. "Richard, can I ask you a favour?"

"Sure."

"Take the key, Rowan. I won't be a moment."

Rowan stared at the key.

"You can get me the Escher book you've been going on about. I'll find you in school and give it back on Monday." Sam pushed Rowan from the car.

"What can I do for you?"

Lizzie looked at his kind face, more flushed than usual. Every now and again, often when he was watching Sam, she saw his blue eyes twinkle.

"I wondered if you were doing anything on Sunday?"

"Is this a date?"

"No."

"Oh, okay. Well, apart from taking Sam to band practise..."

"Be between three and four o'clock. The buses are only once an hour on a Sunday."

"Can I take you somewhere?"

"No! Sorry. I'm going to visit my mother. I'm fine going on the bus but I may not be fine coming home alone."

His worried face made her smile.

"It's not such a big deal but if I get upset my head is still wobbly."

"No, I get it. If you need me, call me from your mother's house and I'll be there as quick as I can. You'd best give me the postcode now." He took out his phone and added the digits and letters to his notes. "Whereabouts is that?"

"Danbury."

"It'll take me half hour to get there, at least."

"I'll meet you in the Danbury Lakes car park by the ice cream van but I'm sure I'll be fine. Thanks, Richard."

"Call me, if you need me."

"I will."

"Have a good day tomorrow. Try and rest."

12

A phone call from Marsha, checking to see how her head was, almost made Lizzie late for the bus. She spent the fifteen minute journey brow mopping and attempting to take calming breaths.

"So you've finally come to apologise!"

"Thanks for the greeting, Mum. Hello, how are you?"

The heavy wooden door shut behind her. She followed her mother through a vast hall with an open fireplace and a log cradle big enough for small branches. The kitchen was dark wood with a dark beamed ceiling, black granite surfaces and a beige coloured range, but opened at one end onto a conservatory and a sumptuous landscaped garden.

"I had no idea you were coming so I haven't baked anything."

"I brought carrot cake."

Lizzie took a plate from a cupboard and laid out four glossy orange slices.

"Half a cake."

"It's Rowan's favourite so…no! I will not defend myself! I brought four slices. One each over tea and two for you for later. You shouldn't criticise, you should say thank you."

Patricia McCartney poured hot water from the boiling kettle into a china teapot, decorated with shepherdesses. "We seem to be arguing again."

"Shall I take this into the conservatory?"

Lizzie looked around at the new addition to the house. She visited rarely, barely once a year but her mother was adding extensions faster than a hotel developer on a Monopoly board. A rickety glass and wood lean-to had been removed to accommodate this glossy PVC structure that not only almost doubled the dining end of the kitchen but ran all along the back of the house and when Lizzie stood up to take a look, wrapped all around the other end of the house as well. Orange and lemon trees in huge pots filled the air with a zesty freshness. Lizzie sank gladly into one of the wide wicker seats. The colour scheme was peach out here, peach covers, cushions, curtains and rugs. Lizzie reached for her cup and sipped, nausea griping at her stomach. A large wooden fan turned slowly above them. They ate their cake with the correct forks.

"So have you come to apologise, or not?"

Lizzie sighed. "No small talk? You're not wondering how my first week back at work went? No, I haven't come to apologise. I said before, we need to talk."

"What would we have to talk about?"

"Dad."

"And I told you, I have nothing to say to you about your father."

"Then I'll ask you, why did Dad start working away?"

"We needed the money."

"But you said his schemes were hare-brained."

"Some of them paid off but he wasted most of our money."

"I don't believe you."

"Well, you wouldn't because you're two of a kind."

"And that's what you hated, didn't you? You hated that Dad loved his daughter."

"Don't be ridiculous!"

"You were jealous of your own daughter."

"How dare you!"

"How did you phrase it, Mum?"

"I have no idea *what* you're talking about! Enough of this nonsense or I'll be forced to make you leave."

Her mother's face was pale, flushed at the cheeks and the neck, frown lines scoring her forehead.

"I'll go when I have my answer."

"You'll go when I tell you! How dare you speak to me in this manner!"

"Sit down!"

Her mother's eyes widened, the corners of her mouth twitching as she sat back in her seat.

"You threatened him, didn't you? You forced him to be less loving and drove him to drink."

"You're a liar."

"I don't lie."

"Not so like your father then!"

Patricia mopped at her brow with a peach napkin, traces of foundation marking its surface and sniffed, attempting to raise her nose above the offending item that was Lizzie. "You're a hateful, girl."

"I'm sorry?"

"You were always so manipulative, getting your own way all the time and forcing your father to look at your paintings."

"I painted in the lean-to, here before the conservatory. It looked out on a lawn surrounded by flowers and Dad's gnomes and gargoyles, remember? Look at it now! You're obliterating every trace of him and me, aren't you? Don't answer that. I'm leaving." Lizzie reached for her phone and rang Richard's number. "Yes, ready to leave. See you in the car park."

"I suppose that's a man. Secrets and bad choices you're too ashamed to face your mother with. Don't tell me, let me guess, this one's an artist."

"I'm not arguing. I wanted you to know, I know the truth."

"What truth?"

"You ruined Dad's relationship with me and kept him from me. You blackmailed him. His release was to drink."

Patricia McCartney's laugh was short, guttural and vicious. "You don't know anything." She spat the words, rising from her chair.

Lizzie faced her, nose to nose. "I do, Mum. I know it all and unless you want me to tell Rowan, and risk never seeing her again, I suggest you start being honest with me."

Patricia McCartney's face reddened, her right eye twitching in disbelief.

"That's blackmail."

"Touché."

92

She was licking a lemon ice when Richard pulled up to collect her. He accepted her offer of an ice cream and they wandered under the trees.

"Thanks so much for this. I've had time to cry and time to think and I'm grateful I don't have an hour of being jolted on that bus."

"No problem. Sam and his mates were at the park so I've been reading about growing fruit."

"What kind of fruit?"

"My favourites."

Lizzie laughed. "Good thinking."

"Blackcurrants, red currants, blackberries, gooseberries, so berries and currants mainly."

"I love soft fruit but you'll need to protect it from the birds. I've apple trees in my garden, both cooking and eating. I'll swap you."

"Give me a chance! I've not decided where to make the beds yet!"

Sunlight dappled through the leaves. They followed a small stream into the forest and sat against a hill, bracken dripping over them and water trickling by.

"How did it go?"

"As well as could be expected. I'm ashamed to say, I resorted to a little blackmail."

"Want to talk about it?"

"Not really. It's up to her now. In the meantime, I have to get used to the idea that it wasn't my fault the father I adored distanced himself and seemed to have stopped loving me. He had no choice, Richard. My mother saw to that. "

"Why? Why would she do that?"

Lizzie pulled at a stem of grass and brushed the tufted lilac end against her cheek. "Because it has to be about her, I guess. Dad and I were close, really close. We'd look at each other and know what the other was thinking. He bought me my first paint box and made me my own easel."

"Did he paint?"

"Before he married my mother."

"What did he do?"

"From what I can make out, it was an import and export business. Dad rented space at the docks. I remember driving there once to a warehouse filled floor to ceiling with boxes. Dad showed me fancy dress costumes, accessories for parties with balloons and party bags and gifts. It was probably shoddy stuff but to me, all the crowns shone with real diamonds and the fairy dust really worked."

"How old were you?"

"Five, no nearer six. I remember some of the people who worked for Dad too. They were kind. One of the ladies hunted through a box and Dad presented me with a fairy dress, complete with matching flashing wand. She helped me put it on and I wore it home, my cheeks flushed with happiness, pinker than my dress."

Lizzie dropped her head on Richard's shoulder.

"You tired? Do you want to go?"

"No, but I should. Rowan will be back at six o'clock for tea and I've not started the ironing yet. Thanks, Richard."

"I said I didn't mind picking you up."

94

"Thanks for letting me talk, is what I meant. I miss him, you see, after all these years. I've been carrying a laden basket for a long time and sometimes, it's good to lighten the load."

"How old were you when he died?"

"Fourteen. He died on my fourteenth birthday."

That evening, Rowan attempted dinner in the kitchen while Lizzie shouted instructions from the lounge, standing at the ironing board, diminishing a clothes mountain resembling Vesuvius. She'd left the washing on the line while at her mother's. It was too dry and needed spraying. It seemed Rowan's first foray into ironing had been her last. Once Rowan's shirts, trousers and skirt were done, she chose one dress for herself and joined Rowan in the kitchen.

"Looks good." She peered into the pan. "Did you put garlic in?"

Rowan, her hair tied high in a ponytail on her head, sucked in her cheeks and looked to the ceiling. "Am I cooking dinner?"

"Sorry, you're absolutely right. Shall I put the kettle on to rinse the pasta? Pasta, spaghetti? To go with bolognaise?"

Rowan's mouth squirmed. They both laughed. Lizzie boiled a kettle, starting a pan with a little cold water on the hob.

"How was Granny?"

"Her normal self."

"Did she hurt you?"

95

"No! I won't let her do that."

"But she always does."

"No, it's just her way."

"Stop defending her, Mum. You always do."

"Do I?"

Rowan nodded.

"Perhaps it's because I don't understand, you know, how anyone can be so deliberately mean. I wouldn't say or do something I knew would hurt someone I loved so I don't understand her. I suppose I keep hoping there's a good reason, so I give her the benefit of the doubt. Having said that, I did tell her a few home truths today."

Rowan stirred. "It's a weird way to love but the world is made up of odd human beings. I read in a magazine today about men who feed their girlfriends to make them fat, on purpose because they want to show they love them. How weird is that?"

"Your Granddad used food and sweets to show love, though not in such an extreme way. He grew up in Ireland with four sisters and a brother in a house with two bedrooms and an outside loo. He never tasted sweets until he came to England."

"How old was he?"

"Sixteen I think and his brother was seventeen."

"That's Sam's age."

"I know."

"And look at all the stuff he has!" Rowan took another wooden spoon and stirred the spaghetti in the boiling water. "He's so lucky!"

"And you're not? Sorry. I'll lay the table."

96

Lizzie spread a faded orange cloth over the table. She'd bought it from the charity shop for a pound because someone had laboured over the sunflowers in each corner yet they looked like someone had dropped a chocolate button in custard. She felt two arms around her waist.

"I am lucky and I do love you."

Lizzie turned and embraced her daughter. "I know and that's why I'm lucky too."

The bolognaise sauce could have done with a bit more salt but Lizzie added at the table and praised Rowan for her endeavours. Enthusiastic with her measuring, Rowan had made enough bolognaise sauce for four more dinners. They spooned them into margarine pots and left them to cool while they ate strawberries and soya ice-cream, sprinkled with cornflakes and nuts, from two champagne flutes. They talked about Emma's Mum's boyfriend's lack of thought about underwear, Lisa's yearning for a puppy and the new life of her good friend, Jess, sharing her room with her nine month old sister.

"She's so stressed! Babies cry all the time! I said she could come over in the holidays and she really wants to but her Mum needs to get back to work so guess who's going to be left holding the baby?"

"Does she have a Dad?"

"Yes and no. Jess's Dad moved away years ago but Tilly's Dad is local. He doesn't live with them but he has Tilly for a few hours at the weekend."

"So he's not her Mum's partner?"

"No and Jess doesn't like him. He's really young, not much older than Sam. Tch, children having children!"

Lizzie smiled. Rowan seemed to have the handle on the pros and cons of extended families and she found babies hard work and stressful. Cool.

"Jess is welcome, of course she is, but give me notice for catering."

"'Course I will. Anyway, Jess cooks loads and is going to teach me some stuff, if that's okay?"

Don't say, I tried to teach you but you didn't want to know. "Great! Let me know if you need different ingredients."

"We can always bus into town and get stuff."

"Thanks."

"I wish I'd met Granddad. You got any pictures of him?"

"I've a couple of albums and videos and some rolls of cine film that didn't make it onto video."

"You've got videos? Can we watch some now?"

"It's getting late."

Rowan shook her head. "Lame excuse. Real reason please."

"I'm frightened to look at them in case I start crying and can't stop."

They lay on Lizzie's bed in pyjama bottoms and vest tops, Lizzie trying desperately not to show her surprise at the rapid growth of Rowan's chest. The 34C bras she bought her in May were not going to be suitable for much longer. The scratched silver TV, balanced on the blanket box at the end of Lizzie's bed, gave them access to the video tapes her father had reproduced from cine film, before he died. Lizzie rarely used the TV but had kept it to play these tapes one day and those of baby Rowan from fourteen years ago.

"Your face is completely round! Look at your chubby knees!" laughed Rowan.

"That fairy dress was bright candy pink."

"With your hair! Oh, I can see you loved it though. You look so sweet. Who's that?"

"That's Granddad."

"Wow, he looks really young and quite like you. Who's that boy?"

"Simon, your Granny's sister's boy. He died very young. I don't remember him."

"That's sad. Do you know what of?"

Lizzie shook her head. "You think I should ask Granny?"

"Maybe not. Who's that? Was it a birthday or something?"

"I don't think so, well not mine, obviously. No wait, look Simon's going up to the table."

"Is there sound?"

"A bit. A lot was lost on the transfer." Lizzie turned up the sound on the remote control. Strains of happy birthday, muffled and faint, trickled through the speakers.

"So that must be Aunt Eleanor, Simon's mother. She's a wisp of a thing, compared to Granny."

"Shame it's not colour."

"It was over thirty years ago."

"Wow, Mum. Aren't you old?"

Lizzie thumped Rowan with a pillow and the pillow fight began. It ended with Lizzie rolling off the bed, feeling dizzy and rather sick.

"Stay! I'm getting you water and a cold compress. I mean it!"

Lizzie wrapped the soaked tea towel around her head, cooling her down and soaking her top. Rowan helped her onto the bed. On the TV screen a chubby little girl in a fairy dress blew kisses to the camera. Lizzie pressed stop.

"It's getting late. We both have to get up in the morning."

"But I've two weeks school then six whole weeks off!"

Lizzie put her arm around Rowan's shoulders and hugged her. "See how lucky you are."

13

Lizzie did her best to avoid Edward Brown but on Wednesday the following week, a young shiny suited man who undressed her with his eyes, insisted she take him to Edward's office immediately. "I'm terribly sorry, Mr...?"

"Blakeman, Marcus Blakeman. I need to get Ed's handle on this situation, like now!"

He stepped towards the main office door but she was too quick for him and stood smiling, blocking the door as she waited for Suzanne to pick up the phone, receiver in her hand.

"Can you bring him through, Liz? I'm swamped here. Get Shelley on reception for five minutes."

"Sure."

Lizzie walked ahead of Marcus Blakeman, aware his eyes were fixed on her behind. His aftershave, even at that distance, besieged her sense of smell and she was glad to hand him over to Suzanne as her eyes began to water.

"Hey, hello! And who might you be?"

"Suzanne Marshall, personal assistant to David Brown and acting head secretary for the interim to Edward Brown and you are?"

"I'm Marcus and you, little Suzy, are the person I've been looking for."

Edward Brown burst from his office.

"Get in here, Blakeman! Stop annoying my staff. Suzanne, two teas. Lizzie, what the hell are you wearing?"

The ground never opened up and swallowed you when you wanted it to. In front of Edward Brown, Lizzie often wished it did, or better still beneath him, speeding him down a long tunnel, back to where he came from.

"It's a suit, a trouser suit." Without thinking, she opened her arms and turned around, her sleeves spreading like sails, the billowing swathes of the short jacket bunching around her waist and the flared trousers below her knees, sweeping the ground.

"And very nice your backside looks in it too."

"Blakeman, in here! Lizzie, I will see you tomorrow morning in appropriate attire, do you hear me?"

Lizzie and Louise met up in the wine bar for what had become a regular catch up in the week.

"Met your fella last night."

"My what?"

"Your fella, Richard."

"Richard is my daughter's friend's Dad, not my 'fella'. Did he say he was?"

"Oh no! He came in to book up bowling as he was passing and stopped to watch. I recognised him from the hospital. We must have passed coming to visit you. He's a nice man."

"As opposed to Matt who hasn't even bothered to text me to see if I'm alive?"

"That's musicians for you."

"He works in an office."

"Richard said he might join the club. He's always been a solitary sportsman in the past, ran a couple of half marathons last year, but he fancied a team sport for a change."

"You know more about him than I do!"

"Sad about his wife. I knew right off he was a widower."

"Who's the weirdo now?"

Louise wafted her wine glass. "I'm good with people, that's all. There's something wrong with Tania, you mark my words and Suz is struggling but that could be the new boss man."

"And you sensed all this?"

"Everyone chats for a few moments on the door. They didn't tell me anything but I could tell when they spoke."

Lizzie smiled into her drink.

"What?"

"You're a witch."

"No way! When did you know you were?"

"From when I was fourteen, I guess. My Dad died, life was never the same again."

"Sorry, Liz, I didn't know. So how do you become a witch? Is there some initiation or something?"

"Depends what sort of witch you're going to be. I loved fairies. At first the fluffy kind. As I grew older, I walked in the woods or round the park, sensing the spirit, the energies of the trees and flowers, animals and birds. Later, I encountered larger entities."

"I don't know what that means."

"For me, they are gods, goddesses and elementals, immense energies and masses of our universe that we have personified. The goddess of the moon keeps me safe at night while her counterpart, the god, takes care of me during the day. This knowledge has kept me safe, and sane, since I was fourteen years old."

"And what do you call them?"

"In a non-ritual context, I see them as Isis and Osiris. That's why I shouldn't be surprised at Rowan's love of all things Egyptian. I do work in a ritual sense with Isis sometimes, but I work better with the deities of Britain. I feel closer to them somehow."

"Wow."

Lizzie blushed. "Sorry for going on."

"No, I can feel your passion, your belief and how it keeps you strong. I'm impressed. Doesn't mean I believe in any of it but I can see what it does for you."

"Religion is there to help humanity make sense of the world and their place in it. Paganism makes sense to me. When I needed comfort and reassurance, paganism was there. Having said that, it's not a religion to me. It's a way of life."

"So how should I begin to get closer to my witchy side?"

Lizzie laughed. "The moon goddess is a good one to start with."

"Which one?"

"Anyone you like!"

"But I don't know any names, except Isis because you said it."

"On a full moon, sit in the garden and call to the moon to listen. Share with her and talk to her. Don't force it, just breathe. The rhythms of our bodies are akin to the seasons, the tides and, therefore, the moon."

"I'll give it a go but what about the seasons stuff? It's not easy to notice much more than the weather when you're surrounded by concrete, though I suppose the leaves on the trees change colour."

"I found a book in the library about the Wheel of the Year. Nature is important to me. Trees the most. After Dad died, I turned to the rowan tree in the garden. Mum's cut it down now."

Louise shook her head. "That woman's done a grand job of denying you support and love."

Lizzie sighed. "She has but I'm not handling it properly."

"You've had a lot to deal with. Don't beat yourself up."

"No, I need a change of mind. I tried playing her game, saying what came into my head and flouting blackmail as a way to get control back. It doesn't work."

"But you know what does?"

"Forgiveness."

"Whoa, that's a tough one."

"Give me time."

The bar was busy though it was early on a Friday evening.

"This is my second night in a pub this week!"

"You're not drinking though?"

Lizzie shook her head. "I don't fancy it, so what's the point? I met Louise here after work Wednesday. She says you caught up with her at the bowling alley?"

Richard's teal coloured shirt tinted his eyes bright indigo. Over better-fitting jeans, he looked smart and she watched his thinking process scurry across his face, smiling at the blush her attention caused.

"Louise? Oh yes, black bob, blue eyes, nice lady. Terry her husband seemed keen to recruit me for the team."

"They love their bowling, especially Terry."

"Not your cup of tea?"

"Honestly, I enjoyed the other night, the four of us but it's not cheap. Something would have to go if Rowan and I were going to bowl regularly so, I haven't wanted to start. Am I depriving my daughter? Am I a bad mother?"

"I hope you're joking! Of course, you're not! You're teaching her you can't have or do everything. Sam has a lot, I know but I do say no, often."

"And of course, I may not have a job in a few weeks' time unless I get my head around this dress code business."

"Do you want to eat and talk? I'm starving. My treat."

"You treat me all the time, Richard. I worry about that."

"We're friends. Look, you know how happy I am that Sam has Rowan as a friend and when we all get together, especially at your house, it's always fun. I miss the family thing. It's hard with only two of us."

"Okay but you mentioned having a barbeque so why don't Rowan and I look into catering an all veggie barbeque at yours?"

"You're on. When would be good?"

"Do you have space in your garden for a fire?"

"Sure, there's a fire pit at the bottom. Sam and some of the lads have used it. Why?"

"Let's pick a day on or near 1st August."

"Okay, I'm intrigued."

"Look up Lughnasadh or Lammas on the internet. Shall we eat?"

The Indian restaurant was busy but not full. With a jug of water on its way, Lizzie perused the menu.

"Fancy going veggie tonight? We've come here for my birthday in the past and I know the veggie food is good. Rowan and I usually order half a dozen sides and have a bit of everything."

"Great, as long as you order. I wouldn't know where to start."

Lizzie beckoned the waiter and recounted her list. The waiter, slim, dark and smiling offered her a taste of a new vegetarian dish they had on the menu.

"One of our chefs is new, from a different part of India. You will enjoy."

She nodded her appreciation and sat back with her water. She was getting used to her new haircut and in her own clothes, her armour was almost intact. Not that she worried around Richard.

"So you booked a lane for bowling?"

"I booked a couple for the afternoon the kids break up. It's a gift for Sam and Rowan. They can bring two friends each. They've both worked hard at school. I told Sam before I left. Feel free to tell Rowan but I'm sure he will have called her."

"That's a lovely idea. You're a kind man."

Richard blushed and fussed with his napkin on his lap. Poppadoms and chutneys arrived at the table. Lizzie learned Richard had never tried spicy food, preferring to stick to mild sauces to avoid embarrassment if he couldn't eat a hot one.

"That's a bit wimpy."

"More than a bit! But I saw you using spices in the Bolognaise and it was delicious so I'm aware I've been missing out. Eilidh cooked plain food, you know, meat, potatoes and veg and my mother was the same. Sam's more adventurous and now I'm being sucked into trying new things."

"Variety is the spice of life and all that?"

"Yes, definitely. I'm not sure bowling is for me either, Liz but it was kind of Terry to invite me."

The hot plates arrived, closely followed by the food and Lizzie smiled at the amazement on Richard's face as steaming, colourful dishes decorated their table. He put a spoonful of each on his plate with rice and naan bread.

Lizzie scooped two large spoons of each and ripped off a hunk of naan bread. "Louise thought you were my 'fella'."

Richard grabbed his napkin as he choked. Lizzie passed him a glass of water.

"Sorry about that. Lizzie, I didn't say that."

"I know, don't worry but if you're interested, she thought you were charming."

"That's kind."

"I assured her we were friends."

"Good."

Richard enjoyed every dish on his plate and helped himself to more. The tiny bowl that had arrived with compliments from the waiter was fiery but tasty and Lizzie loved it. She cleared her plate, mopping up with her bread and sat back, rubbing her belly. Richard forked in his final mouthful and did the same.

"Lizzie, can I say something?"

"Sure."

"Can I say it all before you shout at me?"

"Oh, that kind of saying. If you must."

Richard laughed. "It's not like that. Firstly, I did recognise the man in the hospital, your friend Matt but I had to be sure."

"You've met him before?"

"No, he doesn't know me personally, which is a good thing but what you don't know, is Edward Brown, your new boss, is his father."

"What? But he...what?"

"I'll give you some background so you'll understand. This is strictly confidential, by the way and I'll keep some of it vague, if you don't mind. You need to know but you'll still be cross with me."

"Try me."

"Almost ten years ago, my colleagues and I infiltrated a gang in London and found out about a new 'firm' on the block. Drugs were involved and human trafficking but also white collar fraud."

"Like what?"

"Money laundering and insurance fraud, in this case."

"Go on."

"We followed the leads, waded through the minnows and the pikes and came to Edward Brown."

"But he's a lawyer!"

"So much harder to pin down. The law firm was all legit, by the way but he used other companies to wash his dirty laundry."

"How? What does a company get in return for agreeing to break the law?"

"Financial gain, representation I expect if something did go pear-shaped but of the three companies we know about, he had some sort of lever."

"Blackmail?"

The waiter took their plates, offering to box up the left overs which Lizzie thanked him for. She enthused over the new dish, expressing that if it was on the menu, she would order it but maybe it could lose a tiny bit of the heat. The waiter smiled and thanked her for her recommendation. They ordered coffee.

"Yes, blackmail and that's where your boy comes in."

"He is not my boy!"

"Sorry, couldn't resist. Matthew Brown works for his father."

"He knew his Dad was my boss!"

"So why didn't he tell you?"

"I don't know!"

"Where did you meet?"

"Hang on, he asked me something about the staff when…wait, he's asked me a few times, whether anyone has had a warning or disciplinary. He knew I hadn't…it wasn't a chance meeting in the park, was it?"

Richard shook his head. "For some reason, Matt targeted you. How did you get the job, by the way?"

"The usual way, I suppose. Moving house, I was looking for something I could bus to and I saw the job in the newspaper."

"Where did you work before?"

"A law firm in Brentwood."

"Wyatt, Hughes and Lane?"

"Yes!"

"Seems Edward Brown wants to keep you close, somewhere he can keep an eye on you, for some reason. His daughter-in-law, Rhianna Wyatt heads up the firm, wife of Matt's older brother, Francis."

"But why me? How long have you known all this?"

"Are you *very* cross with me? I knew you worked for Edward Brown but couldn't exactly tell you how I knew him as it was police business."

"You're telling me now!"

"Not everything, I can't, but I've told you because I wondered if you would help me with the investigation?"

"I thought you'd left the force."

"On a permanent full time basis, I have and I'd rather people believed I'm retired."

Lizzie sat holding her coffee cup, mulling over the evening's revelations.

"Good job I didn't fall for Matt."

Richard raised his eyebrows.

"Don't you dare!" Lizzie laughed. "He sang in the park, you know, in the sunshine and the words were beautiful. I felt he was singing to me. I wanted him then. I'm no different from any other single person who's not had love in their lives for a while. I wanted him and I wanted it to be him and me, entwined together, someone to love. That is so damn sad."

"No, I get it. I do understand. So you're not too cross?"

"Not with you. Only my own idiocy. So how can I help? You know I can't put my job in any more jeopardy than it is?"

"Absolutely, but hasn't it struck you as odd that you can keep your job with rules attached?"

"What do you mean?"

"You've been asked to conform with your clothes. What have other staff members been asked to do to keep their jobs?"

"I don't know but...you think Edward Brown is blackmailing his own staff?"

"I don't know but I don't think it's the same for you anyway. Edward Brown wants to keep you in his employ. It would have been easy to say you didn't meet their standards and had failed your probation."

"So what's the plan?"

"You sure about this?"

"Tell me the plan and I'll let you know. I won't put Rowan in danger either, by the way."

"I wouldn't ask you to do that. It isn't dangerous for either of you. Are you a good actress?"

"What role had you in mind?"

"Devoted girlfriend and dedicated member of staff. I need you to string Matthew Brown along a bit longer and I've an idea to help with your clothes too, if you're up for it."

"Hi Matt."

"Lizzie! I'm so glad you called! I dropped my phone in the bath and lost all my numbers. How are you? How's the head?"

"I'm good, head's much better. Went back to work last week."

"I'm glad. I was worried you were seeing that other creep. Sorry, he was so interfering."

"I told you. Richard is the Dad of one of my daughter's friends. He'd learned I was in hospital and was visiting a friend and popped in."

"Didn't seem like that!"

"Maybe he was being a little protective of me. Single mother, wee bit scatty, just had a massive blow to the head. You can't blame him!"

Matt laughed. "I've missed you."

Lizzie laughed too. It was the best course of action. She could lie about some things but she certainly hadn't missed him. "So we're friends again?"

"You know I want more than that."

"Can we start as friends and work on it? I haven't been on a proper date for years, Matt. Be gentle with me."

"I would love to be gentle with you."

His flirting made her sick but she stuck with it.

"I think that's good! I'm going early to the park on Sunday morning. The weather's due to be scorching and I love the morning air before anyone else has breathed it."

There was silence. "How early?"

"How did I do?"

"Magnifique!" Richard pressed his fingers to his lips and waved the kiss into the air.

"I've never been good at lying."

"You were great."

"So what now?"

"Best get you in before the neighbours start talking and I'll email Esther when I get back."

"Esther?"

"My sister. About the clothes."

"Great! It's a brilliant idea, thank you."

14

The park was devoid of humanity but humming with natural life. Ducklings were out early on the lake with their mother, their fluff speckled bodies showing glimpses of adult feathers. Birds called from tree to tree and Lizzie sat beneath her oak, following the calls. Matt arrived twenty minutes late.

"Sorry." He threw himself on the grass and rested his head in her lap.

"Out with the band last night?"

"No, a bunch of mates. Band's not working out the way I'd hoped. Too many egos, if you ask me."

Lizzie bit her lip. "It's peaceful here, time to relax and get to know each other." She felt his hand drifting up her thigh. "I meant talking, Matt."

"About what?"

"Well, you know I'm single with a daughter and work for Brown, Melchett and Brown, but not much else."

"You bake cakes for charity and they want you to wear a suit at work."

"Fair enough but what about you? You said your parents were divorced and I know your Dad is living with you, or has he moved on?"

"He's still here. Mum lives in Spain."

"Any brothers or sisters?"

"One brother and two sisters but we're not close."

"You don't visit your Mum?"

"Is this necessary?"

"No, probably not. I'm plucking up the courage to visit my Mum this afternoon. Maybe that's why I thought of that."

Matt sat beside her. His face was tired but pinker now and his cheeks and chin had lost fluff to the point of being almost clean shaven. Blond stubble glistened and soft lips beckoned.

"Your hair suits you like that."

"Thanks. I'm getting used to it but some days, I still hate it. Glad it suits me."

"You're funny." He stroked her cheek.

"Shall we walk?"

The bus driver was most accommodating when she spun a yarn about being followed so was on the wrong bus on purpose and happily dropped her off by the shops with a promise to put her £1 in a charity box. She hurried back down the long road to the park and ran back through the gates. Richard sat beneath the oak tree with two takeaway cups.

"Thought you could do with a coffee."

"Thanks. Did you get down okay?"

"No problem though it is a longer drop than you think from the lowest branch."

"Could you hear? I tried."

"You did fine. He is a bit slimy, Lizzie."

"Even slimier when you know it's all rubbish. But why does he want to get me into bed?"

Richard smiled at her. Lizzie blushed.

"I meant, what's in it for him? No, that's worse."

"You mean, what difference does it make to Edward whether he sleeps with you or not?"

"That sounds bad too! I feel there's something missing. Actually lots of things but the more I know, the more questions emerge."

Richard raised his cup. "Welcome to detectoring."

"I'm only helping you because I want to know what's going on. You can count me out of any more stake outs." She rested her head on his shoulder. "I'm tired."

"Let's get you home then. Thanks so much for doing this."

She took his arm with one hand, holding him still, before dipping into the pocket of her dungarees with the other. Three squirrels crept round the trunk towards them and sat in a row. Lizzie held out one nut at a time. She greeted each squirrel, enquiring how they were and once in possession of their treat, the squirrels sat and removed the shells in front of them, sitting comfortably on their haunches. Once Lizzie finished talking, they scampered away.

Lizzie held onto Richard's arm, across the grass to the road he'd parked in.

"I learn something new about you every day," said Richard.

"And every day I seem weirder. It's no big deal. I like squirrels. They're surprisingly good company. I went to a park in East London with my Dad when I was little, six or seven years old and I put my bag down beside me. It was a woven bag with a plaited cord. We ate our sandwiches and Dad had brought monkey nuts for the squirrels. They took them from his hand. A mother arrived with a baby who scampered into my bag, peeping out until his mother returned with the nuts. The squirrel mother said thank you, well that's how it seemed, and I've had an affinity with squirrels ever since. They're a good judge of character too."

Richard opened her car door.

"That day, in the park, a bigger boy came over, one hand in his pocket. The squirrels fled except one who ran over to the boy and nipped his ankle. His hand came out holding a tube of ant killer."

"What?"

"Bullies always pick on smaller creatures. The squirrels know a bully when they see one. Richard, I realise you now probably have enough information on me to have me committed."

Richard laughed. "I'm glad you can share who you are with me."

"Thanks and it goes both ways."

"Thanks, Lizzie."

Lizzie knocked at the wooden door. Shaded from the late afternoon sun, she pulled her wrap tighter around her shoulders. "Hello, Mum."

"Good job I was in. You didn't let me know you were coming."

"I'm here now. Can I come in?"

Lizzie followed her mother into the kitchen and proffered her gift, a posy of cornflowers highlighted by three peach roses.

"From your garden?"

"And Mr Brody, next door. I knocked and he told me to help myself. I gave him a jar of marmalade."

Patricia McCartney polished a cut glass vase and half filled it with water. "I like marmalade too."

"Good job I brought you a jar."

Mrs McCartney spread the flowers in the vase. "I do like the peachy roses."

"I thought they'd look pretty in your new conservatory."

"Too hot in there for cut flowers."

"That's a shame. Best keep them in here then."

Her mother lifted the vase closer to her face, surveying it critically. "There are other buds not opened. I'll take a chance."

Lizzie smiled into her shopping bag. "I've cake. Shall I put the kettle on?"

"How've you been?"

"How do you expect? I was upset for days!"

"Of course you were."

"You ignored my apology!"

"You didn't apologise, Mum. You requested that I did so that's what I'm here for."

Her mother's face quivered between surprise and doubt.

"I was upset, Mum. I know you don't want to talk about Dad but I lost someone special from my life when he died, as you did and it makes me sad not being able to talk to anyone about him."

"Is that your apology?"

"No, but I'm getting to it. I'm trying to explain how I feel so you can understand why I said the things I did. I am sorry I was rude and I apologise for the hurtful words I used."

"Very well. Your apology is accepted. I have my reasons for not talking about your father. You weren't there at the beginning so you can't begin to understand."

"I suppose I have to accept that, Mum. I won't mention him to you again but so you know, Rowan and I watched some of the videos the other night, the films Dad transferred from Cine."

Her mother nodded, sipping her tea. Her face looked greyer than usual. Perhaps it was the excessive peach décor.

"Rowan loved it! As you're unhappy to talk about Dad, I thought I might contact Aunt Eleanor…"

"No!"

The scream was shrill and discordant. Patricia McCartney's face glowed deathly white, her eyes watery and blood shot adding to the horror on her face.

"You okay, Mum?"

Her mother rallied. "Yes, fine, yes. Eleanor isn't in contact with the family anymore, that's all."

"That's a shame. Are you going to tell me why?"

Mrs McCartney shook her head. "It's in the past."

"Then maybe I should look her up and bring us all together in the present? Mum, what is it?"

"Why can't you leave it alone, Elizabeth? Why all this interest in the past?"

"It's my family, Mum and Rowan's too. She asked me what happened to the boy in the video, Simon I think he was called and I didn't know, do you?"

Mrs McCartney's lips quivered in her bloodless face and silent tears crept down her wrinkled cheeks.

"Oh, Mum. What's wrong?"

"Don't fuss me. Sit down. Simon died. He was born prematurely. Heart problems developed but I'm sure Eleanor doesn't want you seeking her out to rake up the past!"

"Okay, Mum. I'm sorry. I didn't mean to upset you."

Her mother dabbed at her eyes with the handkerchief tucked in her watch bracelet. "You haven't. It was a shock, that's all."

"Tell me about your week. Did Mrs Dean help you with the flowers on Saturday?"

"Help me! That woman knows nothing about flower arranging! I told her not to…"

15

It was the night before Rowan broke up from school. Lizzie had bought fresh cannelloni from the deli to go with salad for dinner as a treat.

"Dinner smells good." Rowan crunched raw pasta from the jar.

"I've bought us fresh pasta! Can't you wait?"

"Hungry. Shall I lay up?"

"Thanks. There's a dribble of elderflower cordial left. Shall we have it with fizzy water?"

The cannelloni was delicious and Lizzie's cheese sauce had browned beautifully in the oven.

"This is the best! Thanks mum."

"You're welcome. You've worked hard this year. I'm really proud of you. Cheers!"

"Cheers! Oh, a parcel came for you by courier. I put it on your bed. It's huge!"

"Thanks."

"Are you going to tell me what it is?"

"It's a long story."

"Go on then."

"Here's the short version then. I told you I had another boss, Edward Brown, at work. Well, he's insisted all the staff be re-interviewed for their jobs. Don't worry, I passed the interview."

"So you're no longer on probation?"

"Unfortunately, keeping my job comes with a proviso. Once I adhere to it and sign my contract, I'm a permanent member of staff. If it were work related, I'd have no problem but it isn't. It's about me and I'm rebelling."

"Cool!"

"I haven't told you about this because I didn't want you to worry about me losing my job and...cool?"

"Sure! What are they asking you to do?"

Lizzie told her.

"I thought the clothes were a bit less colourful and I heard you on the sewing machine the other night."

"Sorry."

"Don't be and I think you're absolutely right."

"You do?"

"Of course! You always look stunning, Mum, even when you feel like crap!"

"Language. Really?"

"Hell, yeah! It's not my choice, I'll grant you but at least it's yours and not what some swanky fashionista told you to wear. So what's in the parcel?"

"Richard said his sister Esther might be able to help."

Rowan pushed back her chair, her thick pony tail swishing over her shoulders, her cheeks flushed and her eyes shining. "So there are clothes in the parcel? This is better than Christmas! Do you think any will fit me?"

The following morning, Lizzie was glad the sun was already toasting the pavements. She was unused to wearing such a short skirt. Rowan had assured her that her legs were good enough to carry it off. She wore the first dress they had pulled from the parcel, a sixties Chanel look-alike à la Jackie Onassis in navy, trimmed with ivory coloured piping. A wide sculptured ivory coloured creation held back her curls from her eyes, a cross between a hair band and a hat. The short jacket, cotton gloves and square bag raised the outfit to catwalk status. She wore kitten heeled court shoes from her own wardrobe, yellow the night before but transformed with plimsoll paint from Mr Brody, next door. Lizzie smiled, remembering Mr Brody's shed, a house of treasure full of rusty tins and jars with peeling labels, containing those items you might need one day.

Lizzie walked into the main reception.

"Wow! I almost didn't recognise you, Lizzie. You look like a sixties trolley dolly!"

"I think that's good."

"Stunning." Louise fingered the cuff of Lizzie's jacket. "This is the real deal too. Proper vintage. Gorgeous."

"There's another dress. Identical but the reverse colour way. I might save it for Friday. How're you?"

"Good. Were you in time for the cannelloni?"

"Yes and I can highly recommend it. Far less money than a takeaway and with a salad and olives, delicious. Rowan enjoyed it. That's the main thing."

"You going along to watch them bowl?"

"They'll be nearly done once I've finished here but Rowan and I are making a veggie barbeque in a few weeks to have at Sam's house as a thank you to Richard."

"Nice."

Lizzie smiled. She admired the way Louise could fill such a short word of only one syllable with so many meanings.

"Rowan and I are spreading the benefits and yumminess of veggie food wherever we're invited."

"And Richard is fun to hang out with?"

"He is but we're friends, okay?"

"Whatever you say."

Admiring glances and outright compliments brightened Lizzie's day, from both staff and clients. Her scalp itched around her scar and her shoes pinched a little but with so many breaks from the computer screen to see clients in and out, her head didn't ache at all. In the middle of a large document when it was time to leave, Lizzie decided to finish it. A hand tugging at her arm made her jump.

"Oh, nearly had my tea over. Oh, Mr Brown."

Edward Brown's eyebrows hung low over his eyes, reminiscent of a sleepy owl. A smile hovered on the corners of his mouth. He slammed a folder on the desk.

"This can wait for tomorrow."

"Thanks. I thought I'd finish this for Tom so I can check it over with fresh eyes in the morning."

"Good, good and I must say, I'm pleased you've decided to conform at last. Have you signed your contract?"

"Not yet. I need to make sure I can continue to walk in these heels."

"Are you serious?"

"Of course, Mr Brown. How unprofessional it would be if I signed my contract without a thought and then two weeks later, found out my ankles weren't up to it. I need to give this a proper try out and of course, not all my clothes are like this."

"I'm sure there'll be no problem. You can sign your contract now and you can stop worrying about your job."

"I took it home." That lie was easy. Surprisingly easy.

"Then I suggest you bring it back."

"Rowan, can I ask you something?"

"Sure."

It was a muggy evening. Opening windows and doors made no difference to the air quality but merely invited a host of insects in so Lizzie and Rowan lay on cushions and rugs on the grass in front of the Sanctuary, surrounded by citronella candles in jars.

"Granny McCartney particularly asked me not to do something."

"But you're going to do it anyway."

"No! Maybe, I don't know. She was upset."

"Do you want to tell me about it?"

"No, not yet but I'm sure she's hiding something."

"And you want to find out what."

Lizzie nodded. "As long as I don't mention it to her, she doesn't have to know, does she? Can I use your laptop?"

"Yes but do you know what you're doing?"

"Probably."

Lizzie was grateful for Rowan's help. Without her, she would have needed to join the social media sites. Rowan explained her ethics for using the net and Lizzie was impressed.

"A really cool guy came into school in Year 7. He told us all about the nutters and pervs that get on these sites. Don't worry, Mum. There's very little on my profile and we don't chat on here. So who're you looking up?"

"Tell no one, you hear? Aunt Eleanor."

"So what's her surname?"

"Shepherd."

"There are a gazillion of them."

"They have pictures?"

"You'll have to open each one to look at it closer and you're trying to find an image of someone from decades ago. Can I?"

"Sure." Lizzie handed her the laptop. Rowan's fingers whizzed over the keyboard.

"So you're trying to find Eleanor to ask about what happened to Simon?"

"And to find out about her. Is it bad of me?"

"How can catching up with long lost relatives be bad? I want to know more about my family too."

"That's what I tried to tell Granny." She didn't tell Rowan about the tears or that her mother had looked like she'd seen a ghost when Eleanor and Simon were mentioned.

"Here. There's two in the UK looking the right kind of age and one who looks a bit younger."

"From the glimpse we saw, she looked a lot younger than Granny in the video but I think there are only three or four years between them."

Lizzie scanned each face in turn. The younger face made her stomach squirm. "That's her."

"Cool, let's see. You'll need to…wait, this is my account. Mum, are you okay?"

The photo on the screen was dated but in colour, taken at a similar time to the video they had watched. It was an outdoor scene. The subject looked beyond the camera. The breeze was frozen in time, lifting strands of fine fair hair across the woman's face but without doubt, Aunt Eleanor had vivid green eyes.

16

"Mum? Nanny Martin's on the phone. Can you come? Handset's out of charge. I'm going on holiday!"

Lizzie almost fumbled the handset thrust into her hand. She laughed at Rowan's happy dance in the hall.

"Marsha?"

"I'm here, Lizzie. Have I got a happy granddaughter?"

"You have. Is her father coming back to take her?"

"That's why I needed to talk to you, dear. How's your head?"

"Much better thanks."

"Good because I spoke to Joshua last night. He's back in England but is tied up with work so he wondered if you could accompany Rowan?"

"What? I...when?"

"Last two weeks in August would be best. We've two galas in Monaco at the beginning of the month I'd like to get to. Would that suit?"

"For a fortnight?"

"Or ten days. You'll need to sort the flights out from your end. Antonio knows how much these things cost. I'll get him to transfer you money today and if you need any more, let me know."

"Marsha, I don't know. I haven't booked holiday from work."

"Then do it first thing on Monday morning. I'm sure it will be fine. Tell Rowan I'm looking forward to seeing her won't you. Speak soon."

Monday morning dawned grey and misty. Murk lingered around every corner as Lizzie made her way to the bus stop. Today's choice was dictated by the weather but the sleeveless green dress and jacket were a little tight. She worried her black shoes didn't match. Over the weekend, she'd snitched part of the lining and fashioned a hair band. Her hair was growing back. Searching for new growth, she'd been distressed by the bristles prickling her fingertips but Louise assured her it would grow out softer. One day she would have a full head of hair again. Some days she didn't want to leave home without a hat, especially if it was breezy, so fearful was she of displaying the bare skin on her head. Forcing the curls back with a band ensured maximum coverage, she told herself, and walked out of the front door.

Louise greeted her from behind her desk. "Classy. How are you?"

"Not bad. I've been invited to Spain for a fortnight."

"Lucky you."

"I guess but I haven't booked any time off."

"I'm sure you're entitled to some, even on probation. Pop in and see Tom. He's been here since 7.30am."

"Thanks, Louise. I'll do that, thanks."

Tom Melchett no longer had a secretary outside his office, Suzanne having been requisitioned by Edward Brown and

130

Tania, by his nephew, David. Tom's office door was closed so Lizzie knocked and walked in. Papers were scurried inside a folder and Tom placed his horn rimmed glasses on top.

"Oh, it's you, Lizzie. How can I help you? That's a lovely outfit, by the way. Do sit down."

"Thanks, Tom. Glad you approve."

Tom glanced to the door, sweat glistening on his brow and darkening the arm holes of his shirt. "I have always approved. You know that. I didn't want you to have to change but there you are. A new broom sweeps clean."

"You mean Edward Brown?"

Tom nodded, glancing at the door again. "He did this at my father's firm, you know."

"I didn't. In the boardroom he said your Dad and he rescued the company with David's father."

Lizzie leaned forward as Tom whispered.

"It was my father's company. It was doing okay but Edward wanted to make more. The Browns wanted a clean sweep. I wouldn't be here if my father hadn't left explicit instructions in his will that I was to take over every duty of his, including his place on the board."

"So maybe not for the best that Edward Brown is back now?"

Tom fidgeted, mopping his brow with a scruffy handkerchief. "I've said too much. Please forget what I said. It's best you know nothing about the past."

"Of course."

"So what did you need me for?"

"I've been asked by my ex mother-in-law to bring Rowan to Spain to visit her. Rowan's father usually takes her but he has work commitments. Do I have any holiday owing? Could I possibly go?"

"I'm sure you can. Of course we owe you holiday. How long is it for and when?"

"It's the last two weeks of August and ten days or a fortnight, depending on the flights. Rowan's looking into it online today."

Tom stood up. "Let's go and sort this out with Chantelle and then we'll see if Tania can't call Rowan and give her a hand with the bookings. We have a few places that help us out at short notice and you don't find yourself in a chicken shack with wings!"

"Thanks. Thanks, Tom, that would be great."

With their tickets booked for Spain, Lizzie focussed on the upcoming Sabbat, Lughnasadh and the promised veggie barbeque. She loved the stories connected with this first harvest, especially the birth of the poet Taliesin but at this time of year, it was important to give thanks for the blessings of the earth and the abundance of nature. It was a fire festival, the Irish God Lugh being known as Bright or Shining One. She hoped Richard had organised the fire pit.

Early on Saturday morning, Lizzie alighted from the bus with her basket on her arm. A thunder storm the previous evening had left cooler air in its wake and she was glad of her fleece as the entrance to the woods approached.

Within the shade of the lush green canopy, Lizzie gathered rain drops in a tiny jar for future magical work. Off the track by the fallen oak, she shouldered her way deeper. A rickety fence helped her get her bearings and soon, she was filling a box with bilberries. She hummed as she worked and thanked the bushes for their treasure.

Out of the trees, she followed a track towards the lake before veering left where she smelled her prize before she saw it. She pulled leaves of wild garlic and placed them in her basket, as well as red clover blossoms and dandelion leaves. Turning back on herself, she made her way towards the road but near the other entrance to the wood. Outside the cottage, she left money in a battered tin for a bagful of huge red tomatoes and another of hairy corn cobs. At this time of nature's bountiful harvest, she enjoyed seeking out fresh and wild options.

The bean burgers crumbled at the edges but the sweet corn cobs and vegetable skewers worked well on the barbeque, with Richard's careful turning. The salad, drizzled with Lizzie's rosemary vinegar was delicious.

"You went out this morning and picked this?"

"I wanted it to be as fresh as possible. Mr Brody, next door, picked me lettuce and basil. I wish I had time and knew how to grow more myself. It's all I can do to keep half a dozen chickens and the weeding under control!"

"At least the chickens are laying again, mum and the one with the black face, Ursula, has stopped pecking her feathers out. I remember the pots of herbs you grew at our other house. Next door's cat kept peeing on them."

"I should try again, Rowan. We could at least dig over a patch and put in some potatoes."

"We? I'll stick to cooking and eating, thanks."

"Rowan tells us you're going away."

"Work has agreed the holiday and Tania helped Rowan book the flights. We'll be away thirteen days in total."

"We're going to Lakeside tomorrow, clothes shopping."

Lizzie frowned. "Not me. You can get the bus."

"Oh, thanks Mum! Thought you'd want to come with me."

"Six hours at Lakeside on a scorching day shopping for clothes doesn't appeal, Rowan. Can't you buy clothes in Romford?"

"Is it due to be hot tomorrow then?"

Richard nodded. "Your mum's right. Supposed to be the hottest day of the year."

"I suppose I could go into town. I don't need much."

"Good, because I thought we might go to the beach tomorrow, if you fancy it," said Richard.

Lizzie smiled at Rowan's face contorting with indecision. The beach sounded lovely, as long as they could take some shade, and she hadn't been to the sea for a long time.

"Where were you thinking?"

"If we set off early, we can go to Dunwich. Beach is a bit pebbly but they do the best fish and chips in the world."

"How early, Dad?"

"Eight would be best. You kids can sleep in the car. Are you up for it, Lizzie?"

"As long as there's room for a brolly for shade, I'd love to go. Rowan?"

"Yeah, why not."

"Do you swim?" asked Richard.

"Yes, but I rarely swim in the sea. I do love a paddle though."

"And she'll come home with her pockets full of stones. I'm swimming if it's hot. Can I borrow your beach bag, Mum? I'll have to try my bikinis on tonight though. I haven't worn them for a year."

"Shall I clear these plates and bring out dessert? We'll need to get the fire lit so we're not too late if we've an early start."

"Chill, Mum. Sam and I will get the fire started."

"I've got this cool gadget to make a spark. Did you bring any moss, Rowan?"

"No but there's plenty of dry twigs and leaves around. Come on!"

It was midnight. Lizzie's Sanctuary glowed with twinkling candles, orange, yellow and red. She sat cross legged before her cauldron in the circle she had cast.

> *"Blessed Cerridwen, mother of Taliesin,*
> *Mother of all that is abundant in nature."*

She dripped in the water from the storm and began adding herbs, her eyes closed and her mind picturing fields of wheat, glimmering in the sun.

*"We thank you for the grain of the land
And the fruit of the trees."*

She stirred with her oak twig and all the candles snuffed out. Immobile and silent, Lizzie opened her eyes. Smoke swirled up from the cauldron, though no fire was lit beneath it. Lizzie's heart pounded in her ears. She shut her eyes again and heard the music. It was a dashing tune, similar to an Irish reel, and the dancers held hands, smiling as they circled first one way, then the other before taking their partners. The men were red haired, their rangy limbs turning the dance into a gallop. The violins soared and the dancers spun into a blur.

The car park was filling up but Richard drove to the end of the gravel and managed to park facing the sea. Lizzie wore a tatty straw hat, secured with an azure scarf which made her feel like Aunt Sally but kept the sun from her face and shoulders. Sam carried the garden chairs and Rowan the windbreak. Shifting pebbles made the walk a slow one but soon they had set up camp with two large garden umbrellas over them. Richard had brought guy ropes and carefully secured their only source of shade. He'd also brought a selection of Sunday papers so while Sam and Rowan stripped off their clothes and headed off on the long walk to the sea, Lizzie sat back with a shiny supplement and relaxed. Richard arrived back from another trip to the car and dumped a cool box at her feet.

"I made ginger lemonade last night, after you left. Do you want to try some?"

Ginger and bubbles was a fun combination and deliciously refreshing. The breeze along the beach kept the temperature bearable and tempers tamed as the beach filled up with families and demanding children. They watched Sam and Rowan in the distance.

"We would have loved another child, Eilidh and I, but Sam's great. I know I'm lucky."

"He is. He has a good temperament and he's thoughtful. Teenagers aren't always."

"How about you?"

"Another child? Honestly, I've been so busy bringing up Rowan and working, I haven't thought about it. Pasta with Matt last month was the first date, if you like, I've been on in years…and look how that turned out! What about you?"

Richard shook his head. "I'm not ready yet. Sam keeps nagging me, going on about me being old and grey soon and telling me to 'get out there'. 'There' is a scary place."

"He's being mean. You're a long way from old. Rowan's never said anything to me. She either wants to keep me to herself or thinks I'll make a mess of another relationship."

"So she knows why you broke up?"

"No, she doesn't. She asked recently and I told her our marriage had irretrievably broken down, there were things said and done that couldn't be taken back or amends made and I had felt the two of us would be better apart from her father. She seems to have accepted that."

Richard nodded and looked out towards the sea line. "Shall we walk and meet them with towels?"

"I'll grab my bag."

She knew he sensed she was holding back. Memories of that fateful June evening were close to the surface, easily stirred and the lump in her throat was choking her. And that's how Josh kept his hold on her after all these years. While he flew around the world, changing girlfriends like socks, she yearned for the gawky boy in the tight jeans and luscious shoulder length hair who'd stolen her heart.

"It's easy to put the kids first though, isn't it?" said Richard. "So much easier than thinking about one's own future."

"I don't look far ahead. Certainly haven't since this business at work. You're right. I think of Rowan's future and try and give her opportunities and widen her horizons but not my own."

"I know I have work to do before I consider the future."

"Like what?"

"Eilidh and I were a couple for almost twenty years so I suppose I mean, finding out who I am now, as a single man. Does that make sense?"

"It does and I haven't! Decorating Rowan's room, sorting the chickens, juggling the home while trying to make a good impression at work and trying to settle into a new neighbourhood have taken all my time. What are you grinning at?"

"Do you ever believe your own feeble excuses?"

They laughed, Richard shielding his eyes even though he was wearing sun glasses. Lizzie stopped walking and Richard stood beside her. They watched Sam and Rowan in the waves.

"I try to tell myself they get on like a big brother and little sister, you know," said Lizzie.

"I don't know what to say."

"They are only giving each other piggy backs, of course but I've noticed the way he looks at her."

"I've tried not to look. Do I need to have a word with him?"

"I think so but you'll need to choose your words carefully."

"Or I'll push them together?"

"You got it but I have to admit that Rowan's been a lot happier since they've been friends. Sam's been a good influence on her."

"I'm glad. Shall we?" He offered her his arm and they walked towards the sea.

Lizzie dozed in her chair while Richard, Sam and Rowan queued for food. They had the best intentions to eat early but the lure of the sea and the sunshine entrapped them so they supped lemonade and read their books and papers until they were hungry. Why were the days the four of them spent together such happy ones? Because they all got on, she supposed. She enjoyed spending time with Richard. They got on well, really well. But he'd said he didn't want a relationship and wasn't ready so maybe he was trying out, as it were, on her, being himself, or the self he thinks he is now, and seeing how she reacted. She was overthinking, she knew but the only other alternative was that he liked her rather a lot and that was a whole new sack of kittens.

Lizzie and Rowan agreed the chips and vegetable spring rolls were delicious while Sam and Richard devoured their fish. Food always tasted good outdoors. Especially in good company.

"So will you be back for the semi-finals in Brentwood?" said Sam.

"Definitely. Wouldn't miss it. Are you going to play the new song?"

"Nah, we've not practised it enough. We need to be solid if we're going to get to the final."

Richard pulled up in the road outside Lizzie's house.

"We're home, Rowan."

She could see Rowan was asleep on Sam's shoulder but didn't want to embarrass either of them.

"I'll grab our bags from the boot as we go. Thanks so much, Richard. I've had a lovely day."

"Thank you both for coming. We'll have to book up a bowling trip before you fly to Spain."

"You're on and Mum and I will thrash you again!"

"If you say so," laughed Richard.

17

"Hi, Mum. How are you? Thought I'd ring you to let you know Rowan and I are going to Spain at the end of the month."

"Are you going to Marsha's?"

"Yes, she invited us both this year."

"No dear, I suspect she needed you to bring Rowan as Joshua was unavailable."

"It'll be nice to see her, Mum, and I can't remember the last time I had a holiday."

"If I was going away, I wouldn't pick Spain. There are far more interesting locations."

"And they all cost money I don't have. There's nothing wrong with Spain. Sunshine, sand and a swim each day sounds a good way to spend ten days, don't you think?"

"If you say so, Elizabeth but I've been there twice and it was two times too many!"

"Must have been a while ago?

"The last time wasn't long after your father died. Do me good, they said. Help you put things in perspective, they said. Manipulators and conmen the lot of them!"

"Who are, Mum?"

"No one you know, and no one I wish to know any more. Is Rowan excited?"

"Of course."

"I'll send her the usual spending money and I suppose you'll need some too."

"Rowan will be thrilled, Mum but you don't need to worry about me."

"As you wish but you won't be able to accompany me to the hospital now."

"I didn't know you were going."

"Neither did I until yesterday. It's a private place. My new doctor said I should go. I suppose I'll go on my own now."

"Mum, I don't know anything about this."

"It's painful to talk about, dear not least because of the irony, your father being the drinker."

"Mum! What's this all about?"

"Doctor thinks there's a problem with my liver function, that's all. Probably nothing to worry about. Anne Wilson can come with me. I went with her to the opticians last month to sort out her cataracts. She won't mind coming in the taxi with me."

"I had no idea."

"You didn't know, so stop worrying about it. I wouldn't ask you to cancel your holiday for me or anything. I'll manage on my own."

Lizzie walked in a daze from the hallway and cracked her hip on the kitchen work surface. Rubbing at the pain, tears prickling her eyes, she put the kettle on to boil and flopped into a chair. Patricia McCartney had never had a day's sickness in her life, or at least not one Lizzie knew about. Her mother viewed illness as an inconvenience to be ignored and pain to be borne. Lizzie was sent to school one day with flu and had to be chauffeured home by a teacher when she collapsed in the corridor. The news her mother was keeping a hospital appointment suggested something was wrong but what could she do? She couldn't let Rowan down. Not for the first time, Lizzie wished she had a sibling to share the care of her mother.

Lizzie declined to wear a wire to meet Matthew Brown but she was glad Richard was in the next street. Deceit wasn't easy for Lizzie but as Matt had lied about his father and Edward Brown was hiding something from her, she didn't feel so bad. Sitting all evening looking at Matt's handsome face was almost a pleasure but avoiding his hands was a chore.

"I saw some new bands with my daughter the other day, youngsters starting out. Have you heard of the Battle of the Bands?"

Matt shook his head and ran his hand through his hair. Lizzie hoped the quiver running through her didn't show on the outside. Her head knew he was a slime ball but her eyes always failed to inform her body.

"No, why should I?"

"No reason."

"We've talked about my band before. I told you, they're hacking me off."

"But isn't it better to be in a band? Won't you miss the opportunities to share your songs?"

"What are you talking about?"

Lizzie blushed. "Well, isn't music a form of artistic expression the same as poetry, writing, painting or sculpture? Don't you feel inhibited and only half a person when you can't express yourself?"

"I love singing but I don't want to be linked with a third rate band."

"But you played in the past. Don't you just need more practise together?"

Matt shook his head. "I've moved on with my life, my ideas and my music. They're stuck in the same ol', you know. Why are we talking about the band again? Come on, what have you been up to?"

"I told you, nothing much. Rowan and I went to the beach with one of her friend's from school the other day which was lovely as we don't have a car."

"Why not?"

"Sorry?"

"Why don't you have a car? Can you drive?"

"I can but we can't afford a car. Pennies are too tight to add in such an expensive variable."

"That must be a pain. You should get a car."

Not for the first time, Lizzie wished she were out to dinner with Richard and not Matt. Richard didn't tell her what to do or make her feel inadequate.

"Like I said, too expensive. Did I tell you, I'm painting again?"

The waiter cleared their plates. The pizza had been delicious though Lizzie couldn't eat all hers. They had to have separate pizzas as Matt refused to eat pizza without pepperoni. Richard had asked her to use any opportunity to learn something new, maybe Edward was going away or meeting someone important but as she wasn't supposed to know he was Matt's father, she'd struggled to bring up the subject of work. It wasn't a wasted evening. The food was good. Shame about the company.

Brown, Melchett and Brown gave Lizzie a full ten days off so, with weekends, she had time before to organise packing. The charity shops provided two pairs of sandals, three pairs of shorts, five vest tops and a big, floppy straw hat, even bigger than the one she owned. Money was spent on sun lotion and insect repellent and Lizzie constructed a mini first aid kit. On a whim to move to France after a particularly difficult visit from Josh, Lizzie had renewed her passport which she located and packed in her hand luggage with Rowan's. With three days still to go, Rowan was packed and excited. Lizzie was glad to accept Richard's invitation to go bowling.

It was a cool evening, a chill breeze blew clouds across the sky and these soon turned grey and precipitous. They ran laughing from the car park to the bowling alley as the rain bounced off the pavements like ping pong balls.

The fizz in the white wine spritzer tickled her nose and Lizzie giggled. Rowan's face when Lizzie completely fluffed her first bowl, spinning it out of her fingers, set her off again and Sam's delight at his strike kept her smile in place. Sam had chosen a Thai restaurant for them to try after their game and the plates of delicious fresh vegetables, rice and noodles made everyone happy.

Outside her house, Lizzie turned to Richard.

"Thanks for a lovely evening. I haven't laughed so much in ages."

Wendy Steele

"You're welcome. I've had a great time. You have everything you need for holiday?"

"I think so."

"And you don't need a lift to the airport?"

"Marsha sent enough money for all our travel costs so a car is picking us up, thanks."

"Well, have a great time. I'll miss you."

Richard leaned across the gear stick as Lizzie turned her head. Lizzie was certain it should have been a peck on the cheek but instead, their lips brushed together. Seconds passed, it felt like hours, until Lizzie leapt from the car. Rowan and Sam were talking at the door. He hugged her and kissed her forehead as Lizzie came up the path.

"Have a good time, Mrs M."

"I will. Thanks Sam."

146

18

A limousine drove them to the airport. Rowan pouted happily on the back seat at nosy drivers when they pulled up at traffic lights while Lizzie sunk into the upholstery. Her heart beat in her ears as they neared the terminal, panic interrupting the list she was trying to tick off in her head. Her patchwork trousers were now officially her holiday trousers, a role Lizzie had never thought they would play. Wheeling their cases, Lizzie scanned the departure board while the mass of humanity circled around them. They queued at the check-in, Rowan chattering happily while Lizzie pretended to listen. Flights and delays were announced in a metallic, echoing voice, while children cried and seasoned travellers, ear plugs in situ, strolled to their destination.

They ate their sandwiches in the departure lounge, Lizzie treating them to drinks, and watched the seats fill up with holiday makers on their way to Spain. They took it in turns to use the bathroom facilities until their flight was called. An argument at the check-in desk kept them waiting in line.

"I booked two seats together! There must be some mistake."

A young mother stood with a toddler on her hip, a vast carry-on bag bouncing on the other and a young girl clinging to her skirt.

"I'm sorry, madam, but you didn't."

"You can't expect a five year old to sit beside a stranger on her own!"

"I'm sorry, madam. If you'd like to wait, we can see if there are any free seats but the flight is fully booked."

The toddler began to cry. The woman stepped to one side, consoling the little one with soothing words. She pulled her daughter at her leg closer and bent down to give her a hug. The carry-on bag flipped over her shoulder and sent her tumbling to the floor. No one moved. Except Lizzie and Rowan. In seconds, their space in the queue disappeared.

The short flight seemed even shorter. It was amazing how many nursery rhymes and songs Lizzie remembered. Rowan had the whole row singing 'Wheels on the bus' and Teagan didn't even notice they'd taken off. With her tight dark curls and serious brown eyes, she reminded Lizzie of a young Rowan and the memory made her smile. While they explored the delights of the food tray, Teagan told them they were visiting her Grandma and if her mummy could find a job, they would go back again, to live there before her birthday. They talked birthdays for a while and school and baby brothers until Teagan's mother passed by on her way to the toilet and shyly handed over four books. As the sign lit up to fasten their seatbelts, Lizzie was reading a story to a child on her lap and she couldn't resist giving Teagan a hug before she fastened her into her seat.

They waited for the other passengers to disembark before making their way off the plane. Lizzie took Conor and walked with him while the others queued at passport control and again at baggage handling. They walked through departure towards a handsome, elderly man holding a card saying 'Martin'.

"Thank you, thank you so much. I don't know what I would've done…"

"There's no need, honestly. It was a pleasure, really."

The young woman, Rosi, rummaged in the front pocket of her bag and produced a card. "You said you were staying near Ojen. Momma lives a few miles away, outside Marina de Cabopino. She has her own place, a little cottage in the grounds of the villa she looks after. It would be fun to meet up, if you have time. My phone will take a message so I could call you back."

Lizzie took the card. "We'd like that very much, Rosi. I'm sure we'll be able to manage it. Teagan said you're looking for a job, with a view to staying here."

Rosi nodded. "I'm hoping to get cleaning or other domestic work, jobs I can do while Teagan is at school. Momma can manage Conor for a few hours at a time. We need a change. There's nothing for us in England."

"I'm sorry. I hope you find what you're looking for."

"Mummy was a singer before I was born."

"So that's why you sing so beautifully!"

Teagan clung to Rowan's legs. "Hey, munchkin. You help your Mum find the way to Grandma's and we'll see you soon."

The villa was accessed through huge iron gates manned by a security guard. He nodded to their driver, Alain, and the gates slowly opened.

"This is great, Mum. It's so much warmer than England!"

"You still have to wear your lotion though. I know your skin tans easily but that doesn't mean...Sorry, can't help myself. Look at these beautiful gardens." Lizzie's pressed her nose to the window, "And that looks like a pagoda!"

"I knew you'd like it here." Rowan grinned. "You need to chill, mum and stop fretting. This holiday will do you good."

Lizzie smiled. "You're probably right."

"Only probably?"

Lizzie had eyes only for the house. They were almost at the top of the private drive.

"Yes, Rowan. That's your father on the veranda with Nanny Martin."

You couldn't dislike Bryony. Hating Bryony would be akin to hating a new born lamb. Lizzie tried not to stare as Bryony rubbed lotion over her breasts, protruding from her bikini, and over an impossibly flat stomach.

"Shall I do you, Rowan?"

"She won't be sitting in the sun, thank you." The words flew from Lizzie's lips like the roar of a lioness. "Sorry, Bryony. We're not used to such strong sunshine."

Bryony smiled, her grey eyes filling with tears. "Of course you're not. Look how pale you are. Start in the shade, Rowan and with your complexion, you'll have a tan like your Nan's before the week is out!"

Lizzie frowned. She tried not to but her face wouldn't listen. She looked over at Marsha Martin, three loungers down. Her leathery face glistened with oil while two blue circles shone out of it, glorious sapphires in a mud pool. Her bleached blond locks hung over her shoulders. A young man sat on a lounger facing her on one side. Josh sat on the other.

Josh looked older and had developed a paunch, sagging over his fluorescent Bermuda shorts. Grey hairs speckled the shadow on his chin and she suspected the rich dark hair, falling to his shoulders, was enhanced. She looked away from the cause of so much pain in her life and adjusted the sun shade. The young man beside Marsha came over to help her.

"Thanks, Antonio. You're very kind."

"And you are very welcome, Miss Lizzie. Mrs Martin is happy you and Miss Rowan are here. Family are important to her."

"As are you! What would she do without you?"

Antonio bowed briefly. "I do my job, Miss Lizzie and make sure Mrs Martin has everything she needs. Staff can take advantage if you don't know the language and Mrs Martin is a kind person."

"She is, very kind."

The late afternoon sun beamed down. Lizzie relaxed and read a little of her book while Rowan fidgeted. After half an hour, Lizzie closed her book and looked at Rowan. Without a word, they dived into the pool. Lizzie had perused swimwear, bikinis and suits, but declined to purchase a new one so she swam in her plain blue Speedo one piece. Rowan wore a tank top two piece in vibrant red with white polka dots. They raced to the far side of the

151

pool, touching the side in a shower of spray and laughing as they surfaced.

"You okay?"

Lizzie nodded. "It's Marsha's house. She can invite who she likes but I thought your father couldn't bring you because he was busy?"

"Looks like Nanny found a way to get you to have a holiday, I reckon. Or maybe she wanted to see you. You've always got on well. It's a bit weird, though, with both of you here. And Bryony."

"It is but I guess we'll have to get used to it."

"Has he spoken to you?"

"No, we have nothing to say to each other. We've both moved on with our lives and hopefully, you and he will get a chance to spend some time together."

"I haven't seen him for over a year."

"I know."

"He didn't remember my birthday and the token at Christmas came from Nanny."

Lizzie raised her eyebrows.

"I saw the Spanish postmark, even though you tried to hide it. Don't worry, Mum. I know what he's like."

"You do?"

"I know I used to worship the ground he walked on but Sam suggested I took a step back."

"Right."

"I began to see things from both sides. I know you chose to leave Dad but he's always had the choice to be a part of my life, and he didn't take it."

"I see."

"Don't look so worried. I'm not going to make a scene or anything. In fact, it suits me better to play along. I might get some money out of it."

"Rowan!"

"Well why not? You brought me up with no help from him so why shouldn't he treat me now?"

"Be careful, little flower. I don't want to see you get hurt."

"I won't and I like Bryony. Race you back!"

They swam and tumbled in the water. They jumped, knees to their chins off the diving board causing waves to lap out of the pool. As her finger tips crinkled, Lizzie was glad to run from the water and shelter under the sun shade. She sat on her lounger patting herself dry. Antonio called her over. Beside him on his lounger, she tucked her sarong around her legs and adjusted her straw hat. Antonio moved the sun shade and she ditched the hat. All the while, her skin prickled at the force of Josh's stare. Tiny cracks skittered over her armour.

"You're looking good." How could anyone inject so much annoyance into such a simple phrase? What had he expected? "How's your head?"

"Good thanks."

Josh ran a hand through his hair, a glimpse of gold glinting in his ear. "And you can still swim."

Lizzie shrugged. It must have been a rhetorical question because she certainly couldn't think of an answer.

"Lizzie?"

Marsha had been dozing beneath the full force of the sun. She tried to sit up and Antonio was beside her, arranging pillows at her back. Before sitting down, he brought her water and adjusted the pillow beneath her swollen ankles.

"I'm here. I've had a swim with Rowan. Thank you so much for inviting us. Surprised to see you though, Josh."

"Why?"

"I understood you were unavailable to accompany our daughter to your mother's this year, so I took the time off work."

Joshua stared at his mother. "You didn't ask me! What's going on?"

Marsha smiled, her face crinkling like a succulent prune. "I wanted you both here. Old woman's prerogative. And my granddaughter too. Don't look at me like that, Joshua. I don't see why we all can't be a family for a week or two."

Joshua stood, his tall once lean body towering over his diminutive mother. Lizzie saw the frown lines imbedded in his forehead and the scowl marks around his mouth. "I'm not playing happy families for anyone!"

"Sit down, Joshua."

"I'm not a child anymore! You can't tell me what to do!"

Lizzie blushed. Why did her ex-husband continue to cause her embarrassment? "Your Mum was asking you. Why not have a peaceful holiday for your mum's sake?"

Joshua glared at Lizzie. "Are you in on this too?"

"Of course not! Do you think I'd choose to spend my first holiday in ten years with you? Sorry, Marsha."

Marsha shook her head. "If only you'd given this boy another chance, you could have been the making of him you know."

Josh sat down on his lounger and leered at Lizzie. He was daring her to tell the truth. She was tempted. "You know Josh and I weren't compatible, Marsha. Far better for both parties to go their separate ways but there's no reason why we can't be civil. We won't be together here all the time. Rowan and I are going to the beach tomorrow. Josh doesn't have to come."

"Josh does, unless you want to drive yourself."

Lizzie dived into the pool, the cool water setting her pulse racing. For too many years she had worn a disguise, keeping up the pretence of happy daughter and contented wife. After Josh, she was determined to be herself, fastening the straps and buckles of her armour. Clothes came first before she learned to construct a magical buffer, so how did Joshua Martin still have the power to strip her naked? She needed to take that power from him.

Rowan joined Lizzie swimming lengths of the pool.

"I heard what Dad was saying. Why did Nanny Martin cook this up?"

"She said she wants her family around her."

"But why now?"

"As good a time as any."

"Bryony thinks Dad's jealous of you."

"Why?"

"Have you looked in the mirror lately mum?"

"Why? Have I streaks of lotion on my face or something?"

"No, you're beautiful. Don't you get it?"

Lizzie grabbed the pool rail and pulled to the side. "What are you saying?"

"Bryony says Dad has to have his own way."

"I know that."

"It's like, he believes he has the right, you know, like he's better than everyone else. You divorced him. He can't have you and the fact you look amazing makes it worse."

"Rowan, at the time the divorce came through, he was on his fourth new girlfriend. He didn't want me."

"He may not have done at the time but Bryony thinks he does now."

"How does…why would Bryony tell you this?"

"She loves him, Mum but she's pretty sure he loves someone else."

"Doesn't have to be me."

"Bryony says they had a rough time in New Zealand."

"Poor them. Sorry, that was mean. Look, their relationship has nothing to do with me."

"If Dad still loves you it does. Do you love him, Mum?"

"No! I can't believe you're asking me! We shared a few years together and he is your birth father and that's as far as it goes."

"Aw Mum, I didn't mean to upset you."

Lizzie brushed away her tears. "It's in the past, little flower. All the good times but all the bad and the very very bad too. That's where I want to keep it."

"Sure." Rowan hugged her. "But you really should look in the mirror."

The following morning, over breakfast, Lizzie asked Antonio about options to get to the beach.

"Take my car to the beach, Miss Lizzie. Easy to drive."

"That's kind of you, really but I've not driven for years."

"It is beach buggy. Like your dodgem car. Foot on pedal and go."

"Go on, Mum. Be fun."

"Your mother doesn't drive anymore, Rowan. Bryony's tired but I suppose I can drive you," said Josh.

The signpost at the crossroads was before Lizzie. She saw it clearly in her mind. This was an important moment in her life. One way, she would continue to carry the baggage of the past, all the pain and anguish, humiliation and hurt while the other, led her towards an independent life and Josh and his manipulation and selfishness would be behind her and her armour intact. Fighting down the ball of emotion gathering in her throat, Lizzie decided.

"Thanks, Antonio. I'll give it a go."

The mountain road was almost deserted until they neared Ojen. The car was easy to drive but staying on the right was a challenge. Lizzie's ears buzzed but she sucked a lemon sherbet, helping her concentrate, forcing back the panic she could feel rising in her stomach. Through Cabopino, cars, bikes and pedestrians vied for precedence but they were in no rush and out the other side, the wind caught their hair as they followed the winding road to the beach. Antonio's instructions led them to an area where they could drive onto the sand. Lizzie spun the car around so they could access their gear from the back.

"You're enjoying this."

Lizzie pulled on the handbrake and grinned. "It's okay now I've got the hang of it."

Sun shade erected, they knocked in a wind break for privacy and sat together on raffia mats eating peaches. The beach sparkled as light dazzled off the sea.

"This is beautiful," said Lizzie.

"I told you it was lovely here. I wanted to live here, remember?"

Lizzie nodded. "You were so upset when I said we couldn't. You packed your tiny suitcase and threatened to go on your own. You must have been seven or maybe eight."

"I was eight. Last time I had a good time with Dad, that was and I've hardly seen him in the six years since. I'm not making excuses for him anymore. He's an idiot."

"I don't think he's stupid, Rowan, only selfish. He's missed out on so much of your life while I've had the privilege to get to know you. Okay, that is pretty stupid!"

Rowan laughed. "Sam's so good to talk to. He helped me sort my head out so well."

"You missing him?"

"Hell yeah! What about you?"

"Me what?"

"You missing Richard?"

"No! But then again, yes. I'm so comfortable around him. And confident. He makes me feel I matter."

"Yeah, Sam does too."

"They're kind men."

"Antonio is too. He's been with Nanny Martin for years. He says he's her companion but you can tell he loves her to bits."

"You didn't ask him?"

Rowan laughed. "I did, years ago. I couldn't work it out when I was little because he looks younger than Dad."

Lizzie rinsed her fingers from her water bottle before taking a long drink. She was leaning back on her elbows when the long awaited question came.

"So are you going to tell me the real reason why you don't drive at home?"

"We can't afford to run a car."

"There's more to it than that."

"Have you been taking detectoring lessons from Richard or something?"

Rowan sighed, her long lashes fluttering. "And I thought we were getting on so much better but you still don't trust me."

"And you can stop that! Emotional blackmail was one of your father's trump cards and I'll not fall for it again! I will tell you, if I can but not all of it, Rowan. Not because I don't trust you but the details don't make any difference. Shall we walk to the sea?"

Lizzie tied on her straw hat with a scarf before they set off along the gleaming sand. There were a dozen or so families and couples on the beach and she could see inflatables bouncing over the waves in front of her. Once her toes hit cool sand, icy thrills travelled up her spine. Her cheeks glowed and her eyes smiled. The sky was picture postcard blue.

"There were many times I could have thrown in the towel before I did. I want you to understand that."

"You never give up easily, Mum."

"True well, I gave your Dad a lot of chances. I…I was never enough. He saw other women."

"I would have kicked him out the first time he did it!"

"And maybe I should have but your father can be persuasive, you know that. He always talked me round and every time, my self-worth dropped a little lower."

"So he cheated on you one last time?"

Lizzie nodded. "But this time…I had a friend, Paula. We met in antenatal group and hit it off straight away. She lived with her boyfriend. We were about the same age and from similar backgrounds. We were friends for three years, good friends. Late one afternoon, your Dad came home spoiling for a fight."

"And I know why he does that. Once there's a barny, he can flounce off and do what he wants, which is what he wanted in the first place."

"And he always left me hurting, Rowan, confused and unloved and guilty that it had been my fault somehow. Anyway, he went out on his motorbike. I was upset. And worried. I was going to call Paula but I decided to go round there. You were bathed and in your pyjamas so I packed up our tea and drove to her house. I parked out the back, carried you through the back gate and opened the back door and…found your father there. I ran straight out, put you back in the car and drove off."

Rowan's arm held Lizzie back. "I'm sorry, Mum."

Tears filled Lizzie's eyes. "I hate sounding such a victim, Rowan. I hate telling my daughter how trampled on I was. I wanted you to think I was stronger than that."

Rowan rested an arm across Lizzie's shoulders. She had reached Lizzie's height already. "But you are. You got out."

"And ruined your relationship with your Dad."

"Excuse me! After the way he's behaved, he doesn't deserve a relationship with me!"

"Maybe, and maybe one day, he'll see how foolish he's been but he is your Dad. I…my Dad, well when your Granddad died, I wanted him alive again so much."

"So you're saying I should try and have a relationship with Dad, even after what he did to you?"

"I'm saying I didn't tell you any of this before because I didn't want to ruin a chance you both had. What he did to me is between us. How he's behaved towards you, is for the two of you to sort out."

Rowan nodded. "I see that but right now, I can't get past him being an idiot. Maybe I want to see some change in him before I think differently."

"Or maybe you could suggest the two of you go to the beach tomorrow."

"I could."

The sand grew cold, their toes sinking deeper as they neared the shore. Rivulets of water linked across the beach like a drunken spider's web.

"So what happened, after?"

"On the way home, I wrapped the car around a lamp post."

19

Lizzie came down the following morning to find Josh and Rowan playing cards at the breakfast table. She helped herself to orange juice and muesli and walked past them to the patio with only a passing 'Good Morning'. Bryony joined her. Her skin glistened with lotion, wrapped in a baby pink sarong. Her baby blue bikini was miniscule. Feeling like an elephant was not a pleasant sensation or one Lizzie had encountered often. Her small frame was covered and curvy and her breasts were shapely but not big. She took a deep breath and reinstated her armour. She forced herself to finish her bowl of muesli while Bryony sipped at water with lemon juice.

"I'm having a couple of fasting days. It's good for the body. Clears all the toxins."

"I'm sure it does but I'll swim again later and Antonio talked about driving north so we can walk to the chapel on the cliff. I'll need more than water to get me there!"

"We're going into town for some shopping. Marsha said it's the big market today. We need new clothes."

Lizzie nodded and ate her cereal.

"But you didn't declare it! That's not fair!" Rowan's voice reached them from inside.

"Look, it was in my hand there. All laid out."

"But you didn't declare it! You always say, you have to declare!"

"Come on. I'd let you have it."

"No you wouldn't! You'd say I didn't declare! I can't believe you're going to take my money!"

Rowan stormed onto the patio, ripped off her sun dress to reveal another tank top bikini, this time in turquoise and gold. "He is a cheat! He can't bear to lose, even when he's wrong. My second hand beat him fair and square and then he declared nine cards, after he'd laid the first hand! I tried, Mum but he hasn't changed a bit." She ran to the pool and dived in.

Josh leaned on the door frame, chewing a piece of crispy bacon. "She's a sore loser."

"Sounds like she has a right to be."

"Because I beat her?"

"Because you cheated."

"Look, if you…"

"Please don't. I'm not getting involved. It's between you and Rowan now."

Josh pulled back a chair and sat beside her. Bryony smiled across the table at him. He ignored her. "You are involved. She's our child."

Lizzie looked into the dark brown eyes that once made her knees turn to gravy and her stomach flip like a butterfly on a trampoline.

"And this parent has brought her child up well and worked hard for the life they have together."

"Yeah, well you denied me that."

"I denied you the privilege of living with me and your daughter under the same roof."

"Yeah but you…"

"No, Josh! It's not about me! You've had ten years to build a relationship with Rowan and you haven't. It's nobody's fault but yours!"

"Some of us have a career and people depending on us!"

"And you couldn't put your own daughter before other people?" Lizzie stood up and unpeeled her sarong. A desire to punch Josh in the face, to stop him looking at her as if he still owned her, welled from her toes, rose through her torso and glistened on her cheeks. She clenched her fist. Then released it. "You're an idiot."

Lizzie jumped into the water and swam across the pool to her daughter.

Lizzie knocked softly on the door. Antonio answered her and beckoned her in. Marsha sat in a recliner chair with her swollen ankles raised. The whirring ceiling fans wafted the scent of camomile around the room.

"Come in, Lizzie. Sit here. Antonio will bring us tea."

"Yes, Mrs Martin."

He nodded to Lizzie as he left the room. Worried eyes and a shake of his head made her nervous.

"It's another scorcher, Marsha."

"Always summer in paradise," laughed Marsha. "This place has kept me going for years, you know. Sun, sea, sand and...sangria!"

Lizzie smiled. "While you spend all your time planning ways to get your family together?"

"You, Joshua and Rowan are all I have."

"And Antonio and Maria and all your cronies at the galas and fundraisers and all the masonic wives."

"But only you are my family and I'm dying."

"Of course you're not!"

"Antonio has promised to nurse me here. I want to die at home, not among strangers."

"Marsha, what are you talking about?"

Antonio came in with the tray. Lizzie noticed the cut glass tumbler and smelled the brandy. She picked up the glass.

"You've been holding out on me, Marsha. You'd better tell me everything."

Antonio drove up into the hills, towards the giant orange sun. With his battered straw hat rammed on his head and huge sunglasses covering his face, Lizzie had no hint about how he was feeling. He'd held her hand and Marsha's as the older woman sobbed out her story. Two years of denial followed by one of intrusive tests and treatments had focussed her mind on one thing; family.

A sharp bend to the left, followed by a steep climb to the right, sent the buggy bumping up a narrow track which stopped before scrubby bushes and the remains of a stone wall. Borrowed boots afforded Lizzie the purchase she needed to follow Antonio, his hand reaching behind to pull her up after him as they pushed through grass sizzling with crickets and reached rough-hewn steps leading down to the hut. They took off their hats and boots, leaving them by the door and entered the tiny sanctuary.

The weight of history enveloped Lizzie. Her toes curled on the icy stone floor. No bigger than a shepherd's hut, the wooden roof reached to heaven. Tiny windows channelled shafts of light onto the stone altar and the single wooden bowl upon it. Rather than time standing still, it whirled around her. A heartbeat ricocheted around the walls, the footsteps of a thousand pilgrims, seeking answers and peace, across the centuries. Kneeling beside Antonio, a sweet smell reminiscent of honeysuckle tickled her nose. He clasped his hands, knuckles protruding as he rammed them to his chest. His mouth moved in snatched whispers below his closed eyes. Silent tears coursed down his handsome face.

Cool, crisp air lifted Lizzie to her feet and she took the bowl in her hand, deep breaths grounding her to the earth and long sighs taking her to a different plane. The Goddess Brigid stood before her, upon the mountain top, high above the earth. The bowl Lizzie held filled with light, a glorious golden glow of power at her fingertips and she lifted it above her head. Clouds spun around them, the travelling wind deafening Lizzie and she turned her head to protect herself and saw the image in the bowl.

She held him close as they wept together on the floor of the ancient church. There was no miraculous cure for Marsha's ills, only Antonio's love and care to guide her to a blessed release.

Lizzie sat on a rock below the church, the wind racing through her hair, blowing away the shock and the pain. Telephone conversations with Marsha about her dreams, came flooding back to her. Marsha had been calling out to her. She hoped her responses had helped.

Antonio climbed down and opened his back pack at her feet. They ate oranges and looked out over the landscape to the sea in the distance.

"I am glad you came, Miss Lizzie."

"So am I."

"She talks of you often, how you help her and comfort her and cherish her granddaughter."

"But if she knew...why didn't she ask me to come before and bring Rowan to see her more often?"

Antonio gently shook his head. "That was my telling, Miss Lizzie but Mrs Martin put her faith in another. She gave him the love and attention, hoping...I don't know what."

"And now we're here, what can we do?"

"You do already. Mrs Martin is proud of Rowan...and you."

"Not me, I'm afraid. In Marsha's eyes, I should have been there for her son."

"She says that, yes, but she is clever woman. Joshua is like his father, she tells me and she was not strong enough to change him. Many times he betrayed her, yet she forgave him for Josh's sake."

"But I couldn't."

"And she admires you for that."

"Really?"

"Of course, Miss Lizzie. Your daughter might have become more like her father, but she didn't, because of you."

"I hadn't thought of it like that."

Antonio handed her a bottle of water. "You are the daughter she wished for."

"You're being kind."

"No, she tells me this. She loves her son. That will never change, however he behaves but she sees you as her daughter."

Lizzie leaned back, lifting the straw hat onto her head, shielding her face from the sun. "And I've always been closer to her than my own mother. It wasn't only for Rowan's sake I kept in touch." Lizzie laughed.

"I'm glad you can smile again."

"I can because Marsha can and always has. Even with Josh being Josh, time spent with Marsha was happy, relaxing and she was there to talk to. If she hadn't been on a mission to get the two of us back together, it would have been perfect but I understand. I'll only have happy memories of Marsha."

"But not to tell your daughter makes you sad?"

"I'm not good at telling lies."

"Then do not tell them. Leave what you know here, here on the mountain."

"I can't pretend."

"Why not? That is how Marsha and I spend every day. We pretend medicine is vitamins. We treasure each day as we always have. We laugh. We are pretending but we are living."

Lizzie nodded, averting her eyes down onto the rocky ground. "You are young but wise, Antonio. Thank you."

Beside her right boot something glistened. She brushed away the earth and dry grass and a hush fell on the landscape. Skitty clouds banded together above them. They masked the sun on his descent. Lizzie scraped with her fingers and pulled from the earth a perfect globe of quartz.

"How did this get here?" She tipped water over the stone, rolling it in her fingers.

"This place is sacred for all time, Miss Lizzie."

"And our ancestors climbed these hills to be nearer to their gods and left offerings for them."

The stone in her palm warmed at her touch. A vision of Brigid upon the mountain sprang into her mind. They left food and drink on the steps of the church and as they hurried to the car, Lizzie knew what she must do.

For two days, Lizzie lived in her dream bubble, pretending as Antonio had taught her. Wrapped tightly in her armour, she laughed in the pool with Rowan, gathered stones from the beach and feathers from the woods around the villa. She admired Bryony's new clothes and the beaded necklace she had bought for Rowan. She joined Maria in the kitchen, preparing salads and tasting new foods and new flavours.

Marsha was absent the next morning and Antonio explained she was resting, ready for the party that evening.

"We're going to a party? Wow! How exciting!"

"It's only for the adults, Rowan," said her father.

"No way!" Rowan slammed her hand on the table and rose to her feet. "You have to be kidding!"

Joshua grinned. "Get you every time, don't I?"

"I hate you!" Rowan ran inside.

Lizzie sipped her orange juice and looked up at Antonio. "Where's the party?"

"The House on the Beach."

"And we're all invited?"

"Mrs Martin's friends are pleased to invite all her family."

"That's very kind. Tell Mrs Martin to enjoy her rest and if she wants a hand getting ready, I'd be happy to help."

"And Mrs Martin will end up looking like a rainbow coloured yacht! You'll help her get ready tonight, Bryony and you'd better find something for Rowan to wear."

Wide eyed, Bryony glanced from Josh to Lizzie.

Lizzie shrugged.

"Mrs Martin and I won't require any assistance, thank you."

"I said Bryony will help."

"Mrs Martin is my employer. I take orders from her. Thank you."

Antonio affected a sharp bow and went indoors.

"Who does he think he is? I'm not taking crap from a servant!"

"Antonio is your mother's companion and best friend. He is here when you are not. Please leave it."

"And who the hell are you to tell me what to do?"

Lizzie sipped her orange juice, viewing her ex-husband over the top of the glass. "You've been angry all week, Josh. What's eating you?"

"You! How am I supposed to get on with my life when you keep turning up?"

Josh's outburst was irrational but Bryony had told Rowan he still had feelings for Lizzie. She sighed. The workings of Josh's mind had always been a mystery and she resigned herself to the fact they would remain so. She sat on her lounger, her toes wriggling, drawing in her sketchbook. Rowan emerged from the villa and they shared a hug and a swim. Beneath the outdoor shower, they washed the chlorine from their bodies.

"Bryony's offered for you to look through her wardrobe for tonight, if you fancy it."

"Cool, I might do that but I doubt it'll be my style."

"Kind of her to offer though."

"She's really nice but deluded."

Lizzie laughed. "And how's that 'O wise one'?"

Rowan grinned. "She thinks he'll change, that things will get better but they won't. Dad's only interested in himself and that's one of the reasons he's being mean."

"There are others?"

"Plenty but right now, he wants Nanny Martin to give him a shedload of money for some new tour he wants to do and she won't."

They lay dry towels on their loungers and sat facing each other.

"Who told you this?"

"Nanny."

"Right."

"Dad was going to take me to the beach, while you and Antonio went into the mountains. We were all packed up and saying goodbye to Nanny by the pool when she told him."

"Can you remember what she said?"

"Something like, 'I've considered your proposition, Joshua and the answer is no'. Dad freaked out and raced off in the hire car. Nanny apologised for spoiling my afternoon. We talked for a bit and she told me how Dad always goes to her when he needs bailing out or has some new idea. She said he needed to learn to take more responsibility and work his way out of his own problems."

Lizzie lay back on her lounger. "Sorry you missed your beach trip together. You didn't tell me."

Rowan lay back. "Nothing to tell. Par for the course. Dad didn't get his own way and threw a tantrum like the spoilt child he is, never giving a thought about letting me down. Always the same."

"Adulting can be hard. It's not always easy to put your children first when your head is exploding with pressure. Maybe he's in real financial trouble."

"Stop making excuses for him, Mum. You've had far more to cope with in your life than he ever has. He doesn't even have a mother like Granny McCartney to deal with!"

The mention of her mother made Lizzie gulp. With the shock of Marsha's imminent demise, she hadn't thought about her own mother once.

20

Antonio posted their postcards on the way to the party before driving Marsha, Lizzie and Rowan to their final destination. Joshua and Bryony followed behind in the hire car. Through the wrought iron gates, they joined the queue of long slim shiny black cars pulling slowly up at the front entrance. The grounds were ablaze with fairy lights, hanging in streaming chains, enveloping shrubs and small trees. Warm, sweet smells met their noses as they climbed out. A driver took the keys from Antonio, smart in a plain black suit and white shirt, as he helped Marsha up the six stone steps to the open double doors. She wore a turquoise gown embedded with tiny crystals and a turquoise and silver wrap swathing her neck and trailing down her back. Her hair was set in a smooth twisted chignon, pinned in place and studded with diamanté.

Behind her walked Joshua and Bryony and while Bryony's long jade green dress was revealing in the extreme, cut high on the leg and low on front and back it was Lizzie and Rowan who caused a susurration in the crowd. In pastel shades of lilacs, peaches and blues, their cotton gowns hung cool and loose, each cinched below the bust with a matching ribbon. They wore their hair up with tendrils of curls framing their faces beneath a matching pastel band.

It was Rowan's idea to rock the historical look. Lizzie had been nervous at first but Rowan's confidence was infectious. They walked into the main hall, among the glitz and glamour. Even waiting in the receiving line, they evoked smiles and admiring glances.

Marsha began shaking hands, with Antonio at her elbow, introducing the members of her family.

"Robert, Doreen this is my son, Joshua and his family. Joshua, this is Robert Klein, chief of the lodge here and the host of this evening's soiree, the annual beach party. "

"Pleased to meet you, Mr Klein. This is my girlfriend, Bryony and my daughter, Rowan."

Robert Klein shook hands, peering through thick horn rimmed spectacles. Doreen wafted a hand in acknowledgement before taking her place a step behind her husband. Lizzie caught a glimpse of hazel eyes in a face flushed with alcohol and framed by cotton candy dyed orange. Her red rosebud lips added to the impression that she had hoped for honey and discovered lime instead. For one split second, Doreen's eyes locked with Lizzie's and the force of the fear coming from behind them almost knocked Lizzie sideways. Why was this woman afraid of her? They'd never met, she was sure yet Doreen Klein looked ready to run from the room. Doreen drained the remains of her sherry glass and turned away.

Mr Klein pointed at Lizzie. "And who's she?"

"Elizabeth Martin, my daughter-in-law."

"Ex daughter-in-law, mother."

Lizzie's body produced an involuntary bow and she looked up into studious brown eyes. "Thank you for inviting us, Mr Klein."

"Robert, please. Delighted to meet you, Elizabeth and you, Rowan. I do hope you enjoy the party. May I introduce you to George Anders, Philip Bergen, Edgar Masters and Errol Coleman."

Errol was half the age of the others, his blue eyes darting nervously between Elizabeth, Klein and Joshua. He bowed to Rowan who simpered coyly.

"Pleased to meet you, ladies. I do hope you will be available for a dance later this evening."

Guests talked in groups in the ballroom. Most of the party makers were middle aged men in dinner suits, with duly bedecked women in evening gowns, dripping with jewels. A few men stood out from the crowd. Lizzie guessed them to be foreign dignitaries in bright long shift coats and hats. While they found drinks, Lizzie saw Errol talking to a woman in a full length, scarlet velvet dress edged in gold, her hair coiffured off her neck into a creation of which Marie Antoinette would have been proud.

The house wasn't on the beach but above it. Lizzie walked down a crooked path, lit by solar lights and lamp posts, across a grassy lawn and down a meandering, gently sloping slipway, before she found herself with sand between her toes. Shoes in hand, she stood looking at the ocean. No lights were visible from the house but the almost full moon shone over the dark water.

Rowan was dancing with Bryony. The huge wooden veranda jutted out from the ballroom to make an outdoor dance floor. The band played swing, rock and roll and jazz as well as a waltz and a quick step or two. Music drifted down to her and she swayed beneath the stars.

"You're not enjoying the party?"

Lizzie spun round, her shoes raised in one hand like a weapon. "Sorry, Mr Coleman. You startled me."

Lizzie turned back to the sea. The smell of expensive cologne came closer. "It's a great party, honestly but the sea beckoned me the moment I saw it from the veranda. I'm not much of a dancer so I thought I'd take a walk."

"I don't mind. I love the sea too. We lived close to it when I was a child, before we moved to London."

"But you live here now?"

"Part of the year. Since my father passed away, I have his business to attend to both here and in England."

"I'm sorry to hear you lost your father. I'm sure he would be proud of you, taking on so much responsibility so young."

Errol sighed and bowed his head. "I was born and brought up to it but it doesn't always make me happy." He held out his arm. "Can I walk you to the shoreline?"

Lizzie clung to muscles bulging beneath the designer jacket and pristine white shirt. "Thank you."

"What about you? Are you happy, Ms Martin?"

"I am, Mr Coleman. Most of the time. I enjoy my job, I love my daughter and I've found time to paint again."

"Errol, please, but you still have an ex-husband."

177

"I haven't seen him in years, or spoken to him, before this week."

"Yet you bear his name."

"For Rowan's sake. It's much easier for her at school."

"I see."

"He usually brings Rowan to Marsha's, Mrs Martin's, in the summer but she invited us both this year. I'm glad. It's been lovely seeing her and spending time with Rowan without worrying about work, meals or the gas bill!"

She laughed.

"What's funny?"

They stood at the water's edge. Errol took off his shoes.

"I was thinking how impressed you must be with my exciting life. I'm too honest, that's my problem."

It may have been the flute of champagne or the warm evening breeze but Lizzie relaxed, surprised at her openness with a stranger. On the beach, beneath the moon, who needed armour? She lifted her skirts and they stood in the shallows beneath the moon, cool water brushing their calves.

"If being honest is all you worry about, Elizabeth, then I envy you."

"Call me Lizzie. Only my mother calls me Elizabeth but Errol, what do you mean?"

"You've eyes. When you go back to the party, open them."

Errol's chiselled face was serious, his cheeks hollow and drawn. Pain screamed from his pale blue eyes and she took both his hands.

"What do you mean?"

178

Errol shook his head and turned from her. "I'll walk you back."

Lizzie pulled him round to face her. "What's wrong, Errol? Can't you tell me?"

He extended his arm and she took it.

"My father's name was Coleman. He worked for Anita and her husband all his life. Now I work for them."

"Anita is the lady in the red dress?"

Errol nodded.

"Just work?"

Errol turned away as he leaned on a rock and brushed sand from his feet. "I do whatever the job asks of me."

Lizzie sought Rowan and found her sitting beside Marsha on the veranda at the side of the house. A patio heater warmed the cosy spot and they were deep in conversation when Lizzie appeared.

"Where've you been, Mum?"

"I couldn't resist the beach, sorry. You having fun?"

"I was! Bryony and I were dancing but Dad took her away. Said he needed her."

"Sorry you missed out on your dancing. You having fun, Marsha?"

"I love all the glitz, dear, you know I do but my pins don't hold me as well as they used to so my dancing days are over."

"I reckon you could manage a waltz, Nanny."

Marsha Martin took a sip of her drink and looked up at Antonio standing behind her and smiled. "You're right, Rowan and that sounds like one to me."

By the light of the moon, Lizzie and Rowan watched Marsha and Antonio dancing on the veranda. He held her, protecting her delicate porcelain body, gently moving her to the beat of the music, pushing his legs close to hers. Lizzie saw Errol glancing their way and watched his easy gait as he sauntered over.

He bowed to Rowan. "May I have this dance?"

Wide eyed, Rowan nodded.

Alone beside the heater, Lizzie watched the dance of two lives enacted before her. Marsha's was a last dance, a romantic finale to an exciting life of luxury while Rowan's was a new beginning, taking tentative steps towards adulthood, still naïve and still learning but already knowing how unfair life could be.

Food laden tables lined the walls of the room. Lizzie stood transfixed by the marble columns and floor and abundance of scrolls and cherubs gleaming golden in the light of the chandeliers. Jostled from behind, she stepped aside, only to be nudged back. People thronged around her, the smell of cooked meat stuck in her throat and her head began to spin. She hurried back into the hall and out the front door.

She leaned her back on a pillar at the entrance and smiled at the four men wearing black suits and ear pieces on security. One nodded in her direction. The rest ignored her. From this vantage point, she saw the party traversing the hall or climbing the elegant stairs. She remembered what Errol said and opened her eyes. Within moments, her heart beat allegrissimo. She pressed her hand to her mouth for fear of screaming.

"You not eating, Lizzie?"

"I'm good, Marsha. I had some fruit from the buffet, thank you."

She and Marsha sat by the patio heater. Antonio was taking a break, accompanying Rowan to the beach. There was no sign of Josh or Bryony.

"Always a good spread at these dos."

"I was talking to Errol. He says he works for Anita. How long have you known her?"

"Donkeys years! We were at school together. She and Woody came here in the sixties and we came over for holidays. When Howard died I thought, why not?"

"And you know all the other people?"

"Most but not well. Women aren't invited to the masonic dos, except on Ladies Night, of course. Anita's organised most of this though. Doreen Klein is a sweet lady but no common sense, especially when she's had a few sherries. I'm sure it suits her husband that she can't hold two thoughts in her head!"

Lizzie nodded. "I expect the men aren't here to socialise. I expect business is discussed over the dinner table."

"Of course. This may be the annual beach party for everyone to let their hair down but money is what makes the world go round. Did you see that woman in the green and yellow? The diamonds around her neck are worth all of two million. Fancy wearing that to a beach party!"

Lizzie glanced at the gold and pearl strings looping over Marsha's chest.

"These are mere baubles compared to the stones on display in there, my girl."

"Each woman wearing her husband's worth like a decorated prize cow. Sorry."

Marsha waved her hand. "No need, I agree with you but don't be envious."

"I'm not. I wouldn't want jewellery like that."

"I know, but you work hard and deserve a treat now and again."

"And we have them!"

"I know. Rowan told me about you cooking a special meal for her, for doing well at school."

Lizzie blushed. "I'm proud of her."

"Good." Marsha patted Lizzie's hand. "She's proud of you too, you know. Where's that drink?"

Lizzie passed her a glass decorated with cherries, strawberries and an umbrella on a stick.

Marsha took a long drink. "That's lovely." She wiped her mouth on the back of her hand and winked at Lizzie. "Now then, so you know, don't be tempted or deceived by all this, not that you would be."

She waved her thin frail hand towards the house. She leaned towards Lizzie. "I'd bet my last few days that most of the wealth in that house was acquired by less than honest means. I'll not say illegal, because that's what good lawyers are for but near the mark. I won't be part of it whereas Joshua, it seems, is looking to raise his loan by any means."

"What? What's he doing?"

"Antonio saw him with Klein, Masters and that strange man in the funny fabric hat, going upstairs so you're right. Business is conducted at parties."

The odd man Marsha referred to didn't look oriental, yet his attire had suggestions of China. Lizzie had noticed him staring at her, his grey eyebrows twisting with puzzlement and she'd turned away. Lizzie shut her eyes, imagining Josh in a room of black suits and scarred faces, punches and kicks raining down on him as he failed to pay back his loan. Back in the moment, she wondered if she should warn him. But his own mother hadn't. Maybe it was time for Josh to grow up and deal with his own problems.

Lizzie wandered up the stairs, almost springing from each tread, so thick was the underlay and carpet pile. She turned left and up as Marsha had directed her. Faced with four rooms on her right and no indication which was the bathroom, Lizzie knocked on each door and waited before turning the heavy brass ball acting as handle. The first two doors were bedrooms and she reversed out quickly. The third was a library with a vast mahogany desk topped with dark green leather. Two claw footed chairs were the only other furniture. She left the door ajar and stepped in, unable to contain her curiosity about what other people have on their book shelves. Most of the books were old and their spines unreadable so she moved nearer the fireplace behind the desk. The marble hearth and mantel were dwarfed by a complicated painting of symbols and curious shapes hanging over them. Lizzie peered at the strange pyramids and figures.

Book shelves filled the alcoves, most with newer books but some with photos in frames. A collage of faces caught her eye; people cut out of photographs and put together in a montage with houses, trees and beaches. She stared, blinking as one and then two, impossible faces, smiled back at her.

Both Rowan and Marsha were fighting tiredness when Josh and Bryony returned, the former smiling for the first time that evening.

"Who needs a drink?"

"We'll be making a move soon."

"Who put you in charge, Lizzie? Mum, I'll get you a pina colada."

Marsha waved a hand. "No more alcohol for me but I'd love a cup of tea."

"Antonio, fetch a tray of tea." Josh sat down. "I said tea!"

"And I have told you, Mr Martin, Mrs Martin is my employer and I do as she tells me."

"Antonio, be a darling and humour him. Rowan, did you want anything? Lizzie?"

"I wouldn't mind a hot chocolate, Nanny."

"I'll come with you, Antonio. Not sure what I want."

On the far side of the marble room, a door led down wooden stairs to the kitchen. The first person Lizzie saw loading a tray with teacups was Rosi.

"Hi, Lizzie!"

"You working already?"

"Just a bit of casual work while I look for something permanent."

"Who hired you?" asked Antonio, "Was it Errol Coleman?"

Rosi nodded. "I'll have to get on, sorry."

"Don't let us hold you up. I'll try and catch you before we leave," said Lizzie.

Rosi lifted the laden tray and eased past Lizzie. "Catch you later."

Antonio and Lizzie were shooed from the kitchen and a tray promised them if they would wait upstairs. Lizzie leaned on a pillar, the stone cooling her frightened heart and quelling her roaring pulse.

"How do you know this waitress?"

"We met her on the plane coming over. Rowan and I helped her with her children. She's looking for permanent work here; if she can get it then she'll come back here and live with her mother."

"And what skills she has?"

"I don't know. She only mentioned domestic work."

Antonio carried the tray through the dwindling party makers. Lizzie picked up a small pad of paper from a table. While she sipped her camomile tea, she wrote a note for Rosi.

Josh was drinking, quickly, his whining voice harsh and loud in the still night. "You have to know people and that's what I'm good at, see. I always know what they want too. You have to show them they can trust you and you're willing to do what it takes to make a deal or a sale or whatever."

Bryony fidgeted in her chair, silent and serious staring at her knees.

"You okay, Bryony?"

Grey frightened eyes looked up at Lizzie. Then looked to Josh.

"Of course she's okay! Don't you ever stop worrying?"

"I thought she might be worried about driving back."

"What are you talking about? Bryony can't drive."

"I can but you…"

"Shut up! I'm driving."

"Dad, you can't. You're drunk."

Joshua Martin laughed, his nose glowing red in the moonlight. "You call this drunk? I've only had a couple. I'm fine."

Rowan turned her eyes from her father and talked to her Nan, turning to Antonio to add him to the conversation. Lizzie quickly realised Marsha wasn't well.

"You should go in the car with your mother, Josh. I'll drive your car back with Bryony and Rowan."

Lizzie stood up and held her hand out.

Josh stood, defiantly looking down on her. "You are not going to tell me what to do!"

"Joshua!"

Marsha pronounced the three syllables with force and they all turned to her. Her voice was barely audible this time. "Do as Lizzie says."

Lizzie hurried through the couples on the dance floor, swaying awkwardly as they clung to each other. She saw Errol standing by the staircase, talking to a group of admiring women. Lizzie touched his arm. She ignored the furious glares and pulled him out of ear shot.

"I can't stop. Marsha, Mrs Martin isn't feeling well. I came to…"

Errol smiled and bowed. "Your thanks for a wonderful party are not necessary but I will pass them on to Mr Klein. I enjoyed our visit to the beach. I hope you saw everything you wanted."

"I saw…did you know about the photograph?"

Errol looked puzzled.

"What photograph?"

"Never mind."

He held out his hand and bowed over it. His parting words were barely audible. "Go home, Lizzie Martin. It's not safe for you here."

They drove behind Antonio, making Lizzie's brave offer much easier.

"I can drive but I don't have a car of my own. Josh says I don't need one because I don't need to drive anywhere without him."

"Depends where you live. Mum and I get the bus but a car would be handy. I'd like to learn to drive."

"You know it comes down to money, little flower. It's not about buying the car but running it and having the money to fix it if something goes wrong."

"I know. Will Nanny Martin be okay?"

"She's tired, that's all. It's been a long evening. It must be past midnight."

"It's gone two in the morning, Mum."

"Well, there you are. I'm looking forward to my bed."

"I've woken up again. Sure you don't want to sit in bed and watch a movie?"

"Not tonight, maybe tomorrow."

"I'm wide awake too, Rowan. Would you mind if I…could I…"

"We can have a sleepover in my room! What do you like to watch, Bryony?"

Lizzie lay awake, the whirr of the fan merely moving warm air around her. Through the open window trickled the action of a movie and Bryony and Rowan's chatter. She wanted to be jealous, annoyed her daughter was sitting up all night watching films with her father's girlfriend but she wasn't. Something happened tonight and Bryony wanted to be apart from Josh. She would never refuse another woman comfort if she needed it.

The note she'd written for Rosi sat undelivered on her bedside table. She was glad. Asking her to go into the library was unacceptable, let alone snap a phone picture of the photograph. If Rosi were caught, it would be a black mark against her and she didn't need that while looking for permanent work. Maybe she was wrong about the photo. It must have been a trick of the light but her mother's words resonated in her head. 'They said to go to Spain, not long after your father died. Do me good, they said. Help you put things in perspective, they said. Manipulators and conmen the lot of them!'

21

Lizzie knocked on Marsha's door late the next morning and found her dozing on a chaise longue by the open French windows. She roused as Lizzie approached and managed a half smile.

"Pushed that one a bit far, didn't I? But I do love a party."

Lizzie patted her hand. "Rowan was worried."

"I know, I'm sorry."

"Marsha, you have told Josh, haven't you?"

"Antonio, my dear, would you fetch us lemonade please?"

"Of course, Mrs Martin."

"I haven't told him because he doesn't care."

"Of course he does! You have to tell him!"

"Lizzie, we both know Joshua only cares about himself. He's like his father."

"But he's half you! Half of him is a caring person!"

"Okay then, how would Joshua behave if I told him?"

"Well, hopefully you'd see more of him over the next few months and…"

"Weeks, Lizzie. There are no more months left."

"Okay, weeks and he'd spend time with you and…"

"Pretend he cares. I don't want that."

"But Marsha…"

"Tell me something."

189

"Sure."

"What did you think when I told you?"

"I was shocked and upset and I was devastated for you and Antonio, for Rowan and Josh. I felt sad I hadn't seen you more often, as we always get on."

"And did you think about the money?"

"What money?"

"Exactly."

"I don't understand."

"Joshua is his father's son and would only be able to think about his inheritance. I don't want to be around my son when all he's hoping is that I'll pop my clogs sooner rather than later!"

"He wouldn't!"

Antonio came in with a tray.

"He would, Lizzie and deep down, you know it."

"I'm sorry."

"And there you go again, apologizing for my insensitive offspring. I spoke to Bryony this morning. I thought I knew what Joshua had done and I made her tell me." Marsha sighed. "So loyal but so naïve, that girl. Anyway, I've made a phone call and Joshua will not be getting the money he thinks he is from those gangsters."

"Gangsters?"

"What else would you call them?"

"I…I don't know. Is Bryony okay?"

"She is. Says she doesn't need checking over but my doctor is coming over later to see me. I asked him to bring Natalia, lovely nurse. She's going to check Bryony over, do a few tests. You can never be too careful."

"I…sorry?"

"She said only one of them touched her, trying to kiss her…"

"You've lost me."

"Then open your eyes!"

"You're the second person who's said that to me in twenty four hours."

"Errol?"

"How did you know?"

"His father was a vengeful man, full of spite. I only met him a few times. Errol's mother worshipped his father, I know that. She put up with a lot then one day, she was gone."

"Gone?"

"Her heart just stopped, they say. Defect that had gone unnoticed. Poor lad but even all those years under his father's influence couldn't turn him and then his father died."

"But he didn't move away?"

"He did and Woody and Klein found him and brought him back."

"It is like gangsters."

"Yup, and 'family' stick together."

"I've lived such a sheltered life."

Marsha laughed and sipped her lemonade, smacking her lips with pleasure as the sweet sharpness enlivened her mouth. "Most families have a few skeletons in the cupboard. You'd be surprised."

Lizzie swam lengths of the pool, allowing her mind to organise the chaos. By the eighth length, she realised what her ex-husband had done. She forced herself to keep swimming rather than confront him. Using Bryony as eye candy, or maybe more, to increase his chances of getting a loan was akin to slavery in Lizzie's eyes and hatred simmered in her stomach.

Shouting came through Marsha's French doors and Lizzie let the hatred go. Knowing he had failed would hurt Josh far more than Lizzie's contempt. She pulled herself from the water and stood beneath the shower. A car door slammed, an engine revved and the squeal of the skid reverberated around the pool. Josh's tantrum was complete.

Lizzie spoke to Antonio and with his blessing, she asked Marsha, Bryony and Rowan, if they wanted to join her that evening in her rooms, for a simple full moon ritual.

"You really are a witch, aren't you? Do we need to get naked?" laughed Marsha.

"Yes to the former and no to the latter! I planned to call down Arianrhod, the goddess of the moon, on my own but I changed my mind. Your news...I felt I needed to connect with my spiritual side and Arianrhod helps me let go of hurt and pain at the full moon. It'll be quiet time for us four women to be together."

"What a lovely idea. I'm in."

Bryony met Lizzie's invitation with wide unbelieving eyes. "You're a witch?" she whispered, checking over her shoulder for eavesdroppers.

"I live my life with the Wheel of the Year, connect with the natural world, offer up prayers to the amazing universe we live in and meditate, allowing me to learn and travel on the astral plane so, yes, I'm a witch."

"I don't know. I'm not sure I want to summon demons."

"Bryony, did I mention demons?"

"No but..."

"Earth, rocks, plants, animals, the sea vibrates with energy, with life. The same life, if you like, that courses through our veins. Witchcraft gives me a spiritual connection to the world around me. Best of all, I'm never alone."

"I've never thought about the sea being alive."

"It depends how you look at it but one thing is certain. Women and the sea are ruled by the moon."

"Wow!"

Rowan, wearing only her bikini and sun hat joined them on the patio. She accepted Lizzie's invitation. "I've sat in on a few rituals with mum."

"And you felt safe?"

Rowan laughed. "She's not some crazy sorcerer or something! I don't feel like Mum does, but communing with a goddess is so different, it feels like magic, for sure. I always feel relaxed and happy after. Our ancestors revered the sun and moon, you know, understanding a good relationship was vital for their crops and animals and children. Don't you ever sit outside and look at the stars?"

Bryony blushed. "Not really. Josh doesn't...well, he's not interested in that sort of thing."

"But this isn't about Dad. It's about you."

Bryony's pretty lips set firm. "Then I'd like to come along and learn something."

The evening air hung warm and moist, tinged with the scent of jasmine. The women gathered on Lizzie's balcony, beneath the Corn Moon, and gazed up at the night sky. Wisps of clouds covered part of the moon but she blazed upon them, magnificent at her ripest best.

> *"Blessed Arianrhod of the Silver Wheel*
> *We welcome you with love in our hearts.*
> *Bright and beautiful,*
> *Verdant mother of the sky*
> *We call you to our rite.*
>
> *We cast our circle on the earth,*
> *Isis veiled, Isis unveiled are you,*
> *As above and so below*
> *Look with kindness and wisdom*
> *Upon our rite.*
>
> *Fruitful mother, star goddess*
> *Arianrhod, we call to you*
> *Women of the earth*
> *Bound by blood and love*
> *We welcome you to our rite."*

With Lizzie's voice to guide them, three women performed their full moon ritual. First, they thought of the sea, rolling waves leading to crashing breakers, ending with soft ripples in a gentle cove. Here they rested, the water cradling them, cleansing their bodies and washing away the angst and heartaches they carried.

Sat at the altar, a table from Lizzie's room covered with a white cloth, the women gazed at the objects before them. The white candle spluttered at their breath, illuminating two smooth stones, the quartz pebble Lizzie found by the chapel, a large bowl of water and a rough wooden carved owl.

Lizzie lifted the owl to the moon and whispered.

"Blessed mother, hear our prayers."

Where before the whining of insects and the occasional beep of a car horn had met their ears, now a comfortable silence fell. Without permission, the women smiled at each other and set upon their task of committing their burdens to paper. Titian flames consumed each one. 'I'm letting go' they whispered. Tears fell on hot cheeks. They wept and hugged until finally, with the bowl in Marsha's lap, they immersed their hands together. Lizzie clasped the quartz pebble.

"Blessed Arianrhod,
Mother of birth and rebirth
Take away the pain we feel,
Bless each of us
And make us new."

Arm in arm, Lizzie walked Rowan to her bedroom.

"That was cool, Mum."

"Wasn't it?"

"Nanny looked so content. It felt like family, didn't it? Even with Bryony."

"It did. Bryony looked happy. How about you?"

"I enjoy doing something 'all girls together' but it's only psychology, isn't it? Relax, think of all the bad stuff, write it down, burn it and it's gone. Life isn't that easy."

"No, it's not easy but we enjoyed our time together, we did no harm and maybe we can all start with a clean sheet tomorrow. When I talk to the moon, I'm sharing my burden. It doesn't seem as heavy after."

Rowan hugged her at the door. "Give Nanny my love and tell her sweet dreams."

"I didn't say…"

Rowan laughed. "It's not magic. I know you well."

Did Rowan know Marsha was dying? Lizzie lay awake, the airy notes of a wooden wind chime rising up from the garden, keeping her company. She shivered, burying her nose in the sweet soft cotton. No, Rowan knew Lizzie cared about Marsha, that's all. She was snoring softly when Lizzie knocked, Antonio easing into the hallway so as not to disturb his love.

"She is happy and sleeping easily. Whatever you did was good for her."

"Thank you, Antonio. Once we're gone, she can look at the moon and know we are with her."

She had hugged Antonio before trotting down the stairs, grabbing a glass of water from the kitchen on her way to the garden. Bryony sat on the stone wall between the greenery and the pool. Her tear stained face shone in the moonlight. Lizzie sat beside her and put an arm around her shoulder and gave it a squeeze before moving away slightly, giving Bryony space.

"Thanks, Lizzie. I…You and Rowan have been so kind to me. And Marsha. I've been so blinkered. I can see that now."

"Sometimes you need to step away from a situation to see it for what it really is."

Bryony nodded. "And what I have with Josh isn't a relationship. He thinks it is and I did too but not anymore."

"I lived with Josh for years and never managed to work out how he thinks. His mind works in such a different way to mine but perhaps that's what his clients like. I'd never go to see a life coach. I'll work out my own life, thank you very much, but I know a lot of people do."

"He seemed so focussed, so assured about everything but it's lies. As long as he's always right and has money and people to adore him, he's reasonably pleasant but he's less balanced than most of his clients when it comes to dealing with the problems and pressures of real life."

"And you?"

"I was struggling with bereavement and self-confidence when we met. It was easy to follow someone like him."

"And now?"

"If I'm going to follow, I need to know why. What's in it for me? More than that, Josh says he loves me. I don't believe him."

"And do you…love him?"

Bryony dropped her head. "I don't know."

"Then take time for yourself, think about what you want from your life and decide if Josh fits into your plan. Your life is about you. It's not for anyone else to manipulate."

"Thanks, Lizzie. I better get back before Rowan falls asleep. You coming up?"

Lizzie hugged Bryony. "You go. I'm having a final few minutes in the garden with the moon."

Beneath the silver orb, cross legged on the brittle, sun shrivelled grass, Lizzie allowed the turmoil in her mind to be touched by Arianrhod's gentle caresses. Faces tumbled through her thoughts. Her mother sneered and became an old wizened woman in a chair before the fire. Josh barked and snarled and was consigned to a duck pond. Louise greeted her beneath the oak tree in the park. Surrounded by expectant squirrels, Louise's laugh filled her head. Rowan danced with Errol but she was older, taller and more elegant. She bent him to her with her gaze. Edward Brown wore a collar and leash and danced naked on a piano while his nephew, David, struck up a discordant tune. Sam, blond hair streaming from his head, led the band at Wembley, thousands of fans shouting his name. Antonio held Marsha in his arms, forcing life into her with his own breath. The final face was Richard. Gentle, worried and kind, he held off a runaway train with one hand to protect her.

Her prayer to Arianrhod had been to cut the cord between her and Josh, however painful it was, yet other people stood in the way of her happiness as well as her ex-husband. Alone in her bed Lizzie turned over, ruffling up her pillow beneath her cheek. But Josh was the first step and she had taken it. Tears dampened the thick cool cotton before she drifted off into a restless sleep.

22

Lizzie and Rowan were eating breakfast the next morning, soft sweet rolls with jam and honey when Antonio came onto the patio with Rosi and Teagan. While Teagan enjoyed the rolls, Lizzie and Rosi moved onto the loungers with coffee.

"I didn't know you knew Antonio."

"He knows Momma. He came to talk to me this morning about a job, here with Mrs Martin."

"Really?"

"I'm a nurse and he says Mrs Martin isn't well. Sometimes, he is up all night with her and worries he will fall asleep. He needs someone to help out."

"And you would do that?"

"I can do some nights and some days, he says. He speaks to Momma. She doesn't want me to go back to the House on the Beach."

"So this will be permanent?"

"I'm not going back home."

"Does Teagan know?"

"Not yet. I've a friend, Melissa who will pack up for me. I can afford one crate to be shipped. We don't have much but we could do with more of Teagan's clothes and toys and some of my books, documents and files. I rang the landlord and gave a month's notice and Antonio says I can start now as I'll need to find money for the final month's rent."

"What were you doing in England?"

"Agency nursing but only when Mel could sit the kids. I've been studying too and passed my final book keeping exams last month. Numbers used to scare me but there are rules in book keeping." She sipped her drink. "Nursing is still more rewarding than numbers though."

"This position sounds perfect for you then but you do know how sick Mrs Martin is?"

"Antonio told me. I'm so sorry, Lizzie."

Lizzie sucked down the lump in her throat. "Thanks, Rosi but Rowan doesn't know and Mrs Martin wants to keep it like that."

"Sure, no problem.

Lizzie and Rowan developed a routine during the second week of their stay. They swam lengths each morning, joined by Bryony on the second day, with a sheepish admission to not being able to swim. Rowan took on the role of teacher so during the afternoons, while Lizzie visited Marsha, Bryony learned to swim. She'd admitted to Lizzie, the men hadn't hurt her but she'd been shocked Josh would use her that way. The realisation he would do anything to further his business plans had frightened her. Learning to swim was her first challenge, taking charge of her own life and doing something for her.

After her midday rest, Marsha lay beside the pool or on her chaise longue in the window of her room. On their penultimate day, Lizzie took a shoe box wrapped in a blue scarf to Marsha's room.

"Hello, love. Have you eaten?"

"Maria made me a salad, thank you."

"You've lost weight since you've been here."

"Have I?" Lizzie looked down at her body and held out her arms.

Marsha smiled and shook her head. "I bet you've not looked in the mirror since you've been here."

Lizzie blushed. "As it happens, I've noticed myself doing it recently. There are a lot of mirrors in this house!"

Marsha laughed. "Because unlike you, I'm a vain old bird!"

Lying on her chaise in a long peach chiffon robe, Marsha's hair was pinned up and her lipstick primed.

Lizzie smiled. "I've something for you." She held up the box.

"Now I gave you money for the town to spend on yourself not on me."

"We've not been in for souvenirs yet. Thought we'd go tomorrow but I've made this for you. It won't heal you, and how I wish it would, but it will help, if you're willing."

When Antonio came in from his swim, Lizzie had set out the portable altar, the quartz crystal sitting in a wooden bowl in the middle.

"We charged the quartz on the full moon, remember. It's a powerful stone for gaining clarity, linked with the third eye." She touched the middle of her forehead. "But it's also the Master Healer. It's said to be able to draw out pain. From what you've told me, there's going to be more pain."

"And I hate the woozy feeling from the drugs. Maybe one day I'll be happy to be doped up and 'out of it', but not yet."

"You can pack all this away and get it out to use it but I feel it should stay out now, for a few days at least. You could set it up on a small table. The crystal is fully charged so you can use it whenever you need. To charge it up, leave it exposed to moonlight with the tea light burning and the frankincense in the burner or it can be rinsed in the sea beneath a waxing or full moon. Well, that's how I would do it."

Antonio sat on the floor beside Lizzie, watching Marsha rolling the crystal around in her palm.

"Could I bring sea water here, in case I cannot get to the ocean?"

Lizzie touched his arm. "You do whatever you think is best."

"She will feel you here with her, Miss Lizzie and that will soothe her."

"As will you. Rosi will be a great help and give you a break every now and then. Everyone needs to rest."

Antonio nodded and looked up at Marsha. Her eyes were shut, a peaceful smile lingering on her lips and a gentle snore purring from between them. In her left hand, she clasped the crystal to her chest.

The plan was to get up early and to drive Rowan and Bryony into town for shopping but Josh's return in the middle of the night thwarted Lizzie's preparations. Finding Bryony absent from his bed, Josh had found her in Rowan's room and a row broke out. Lizzie and Antonio arrived at the same time to quell it.

"Please, Mr Martin. You will wake your mother."

Antonio's quiet insistence made no impression.

"Shut *up*, the lot of you!"

Lizzie's words worked on her daughter. Rowan sat down on her bed and Bryony wriggled free of Josh's grasp and joined her.

"Since when…"

"Shut up!" hissed Lizzie. "Sorry, Antonio. We'll sort this out, thanks."

With his customary bow, Antonio left.

"I want to know…"

"Dad! Shut up! You know Nanny's not well!" hissed Rowan.

Josh, unshaven and sweaty, pointed a finger at Rowan.

"And don't you dare start on Rowan!" hissed Bryony.

Three pairs of eyes stared at her. She blushed. "I'm sick of your behaviour, Josh. You don't care about anyone but yourself."

"How can you say that? I need to make this venture work for us, baby. For our future."

Doubt flickered across Bryony's face. Then resolve.

"You stormed off without a word. You'd let those men…" Bryony looked at Rowan. "You knew I was upset but you didn't even think about me so Rowan invited me for a sleepover movie night and I've been sleeping in here ever since."

"Now look here…"

"Shut up, I'm not finished," hissed Bryony.

Lizzie struggled to supress a smile.

"You can't storm around and expect to get your own way all the time! Because you wanted me in your bed you've woken everyone up, including your own daughter. That's arrogant and selfish."

"And thoughtless, Dad. All Nanny wanted was for us to be nice to each other for two weeks and you couldn't do it."

"I was…I wanted…"

"Admit it, Dad."

"Why does it always have to be about your Nan!"

"Because it's her house and she invited us, Dad. And why not? Why can't we spend part of our holiday pleasing Nanny?"

Pride glowed from Lizzie's cheeks.

"I'm too tired to argue. Bryony, go to our room and let these people get some sleep."

"You're such a charmer, Dad."

"Now, look here…"

"No, Josh. You're out of order. We need to talk but it's late. Go to bed and we'll talk in the morning."

Josh stood up and grabbed Bryony's arm. Rowan held on tightly to the other and Lizzie stepped in.

"You've got your answer, Josh now get out."

"Just go, Dad!"

The three women winced as the bedroom door slammed behind him.

It was midday by the time they parked up. Three women in straw sombreros swaggered into town. Bryony had left a note for Josh, saying she would be back at three o'clock to talk to him, as he wasn't awake to speak to. Her cheeks were glowing and since her twice daily swimming lessons, her appetite had increased. Lizzie was pleased to see flesh covering her bones. Rowan had grown, in stature and maturity. Lizzie watched her buying three peaches with her practised Spanish.

Lizzie bought embroidered bags for Louise and herself and a delicate chain with a pale blue butterfly pendant as she had an idea her mother liked them. A yellow citrine on a green cord was acquired for Marsha and a t-shirt for Sam. It was black and rude but funny. Two hair scarves for Maria went in the bag with a dozen fridge magnets for the girls at work and her spare gift box at home.

Only Richard and Antonio were left to buy for. Bryony and Rowan were trying on clothes so Lizzie wandered down a narrow street behind the square and smiled at an old woman with no teeth who was nursing a baby on the steps of her house. She beckoned Lizzie and held up the baby to her.

"Sorry? Do you want me to help?"

The woman brought the baby to her breast and shook her head.

In broken English she said. "Your gift, your present for man. He wants child."

They sat beneath faded umbrellas, drinking coffee, their final drink before leaving town.

"Since when did you start liking coffee?"

"Since here! I don't have much, don't worry. Bryony says a tiny cup goes a long way. Did you get all your gifts?"

"Yeah, all spent out. How about you?"

"I got the coolest t-shirt for Sam but you won't like it."

"Why's that?"

"It's pretty rude."

"Show."

Rowan brought out the t-shirt. Lizzie pulled its twin from her bag.

"No way! How cool is that! Mind you, one of us is going to have to get our money back and find something else but I saw other stuff I know he'll like, don't worry. You keep yours, Mum. That's a big bag."

"I know and it'll have to be hand luggage!"

"For Richard?"

Lizzie nodded.

"Richard?" asked Bryony.

"Remember Sam who I was telling you about? Richard is his Dad. Mum and Richard are friends."

"And the pair of you can stop looking at me like that! I've been flitting around like a Mexican jumping bean with all this worry at work and Richard is still grieving for his wife. We need a good friend, nothing more."

Bryony sipped the last dregs of thick black coffee from the bottom of her cup. "I think I've decided what I'm going to do but I wanted to talk to you both first. Can we keep in touch, when we get back to England?"

"Why wouldn't we?"

"Because I'm leaving your Dad."

"Oh."

"You sure about this, Bryony? You haven't talked to him yet."

"I'm twenty four, Lizzie. I've done nothing but follow Josh around for the past two years and for what? It's time I had my own life. You've both shown me that."

"What will you do? Do you have a place to stay? She could stay with us, couldn't she Mum?"

"That's kind of you but I can stay with my brother in London while Josh and I thrash out some details. We weren't married but Josh has lost most of my inheritance on failed tours and bad investments. I've paid the rent on our flat, paid for everything in fact, always with the promise he will make so much more and pay me back. Patrick, my brother, is a lawyer. I spoke to him this morning. He'll help me."

"When are you due to fly back?"

"Next week sometime but Marsha said I can stay as long as I want. She's been so kind."

"We could get the train to London and visit, couldn't we mum?"

"Definitely. I hope everything works out for you."

"I'm starving. Can we get some food?"

"Maria is making us vegetarian paella for dinner and some sort of trifle cake. Have some fruit."

"I'll get some more of those peaches." Rowan stood up. "You coming, Bryony?"

"Sure."

They ate their last meal together at a long table. Marsha insisted Antonio and Maria joined them and with Rosi,

Teagan and Conor invited too, laughter and chatter resounded from the sun bleached villa. Conor sat happily on Lizzie's lap, chomping on a stick of celery and dipping his chubby fingers into his bowl of paella before licking it off. Teagan beamed between Bryony and Rowan, spooning in food from her plate and popping tiny tomatoes in her mouth.

Josh sat adjacent to his mother, opposite Antonio. Before dessert Lizzie rose to her feet, handing Conor to his mother.

"I wanted to say 'thank you' to Marsha for inviting us to her home and to Antonio and Maria for looking after us so well. We've visited new places and made new friends and had a lovely holiday. Thank you."

The table raised their glasses. "Cheers!" Lizzie sat down.

"You're all welcome anytime, dear. It's been lovely to see you all and spend time with you."

"We'll make it an annual event, shall we? Joshua and his failed relationships!"

Marsha turned to Josh, the glint in her eye making Lizzie's heart beat faster.

"Take a look at yourself, Joshua. You can't keep blaming other people. When you look in the mirror, do you see the man you want to be?"

"What do you mean?"

"This isn't the time to argue and I won't but think on this. Lizzie is proud of Rowan."

"So am I!"

"So why not make me proud, son?"

"I get dessert."

"I'll help you, Maria."

"Thank you, Miss Lizzie."

"We can gather these plates, Maria. Will you help me, Rowan?"

Josh pushed back his chair.

"Leave that, Lizzie. I need to talk to you."

"Not now, Josh. I'm not spoiling my last moments here."

"I don't want to argue."

"Then leave it. Maybe we'll talk another time."

"See! I try to be reasonable and that's the thanks I get!"

"Mum doesn't want to talk now, Dad and I don't blame her. We've had a happy day. Don't spoil it."

"I'm not spoiling anything! Why aren't you saying that to your mother? She's the one who's wrecked my relationship!"

Rosi left the room with Maria, pulling a reluctant Teagan behind her.

"You did that all by yourself, Josh." Bryony's face was flushed but determined. "Marsha's right. You've no one to blame but yourself."

Josh slumped back in his chair. "Happy, Lizzie, now you've turned everyone against me?"

Unbidden tears scoured Lizzie's eyes. "All we ever do is love you, Josh and you take it and murder it, hacking it to pieces with lies and deceit. Soon, there'll be no one left and it makes me sad to think how lonely you'll be."

"I don't need your pity!" Josh stormed down the table towards Lizzie.

Fear rose like a tiger through her veins and her chair fell backwards as she tried to turn and run. Josh grabbed her arm and the world turned slow motion. She heard a grunt issue from her mouth as her back hit the wall. Blood shot eyes glared at her. A yell issued from Josh's lips as he brought his right arm back. Rowan's screams echoed in her head. A lightening blow spun Josh's arm back. A crunch echoed around the room as Antonio's fist connected with Josh's nose.

They sat hand in hand in the departure lounge, eyes blank and lips trembling. Josh was spending the night in a police cell at Marsha's request. Instead of a loyal son to support her in her final weeks, Antonio and Rosi would be with her. Josh couldn't even be trusted with the truth of his mother's illness. Lizzie fought back tears of indignation and sadness.

They moved into the queue as their row was called, shuffling forward to present their boarding cards. The sun had shone and they'd swum and laughed and rolled in the surf and sculptured dragons in the sand and one day, they would remember this holiday as a good one but now, as they boarded the plane and took their seats both women knew Joshua Martin had spoiled it.

Tired and grumpy, Lizzie dragged their bags from the carousel and hurried Rowan towards the exit. She sent a prayer ahead for their driver to be there to meet them.

Rowan saw Sam first and ran squealing towards him. Lizzie saw Richard. Without hesitation, she did the same but without the noise. Enclosed in his arms, tears were unleashed and she was happy to be led from the building but Richard steered them towards a coffee shop. He plopped her onto a seat. She rifled through her bag for tissues and spun her head around but couldn't see Rowan or Sam. Breathing was difficult, panic rang in her ears and she bit her lip fiercely, the pain startling her as she blew her nose.

Richard put a small cup in front of her. "Drink. I've had them put a drop of cold water in so, go for it."

Lizzie took a sip. Strong, black coffee woke her mouth and shivered through her body.

"Sam's outside with Rowan. I wasn't expecting you to know already. Did the police contact you?"

"Police? Has something happened to Josh?"

"Josh?"

"Why else would the police contact me? Richard, what's going on?"

Lizzie whined the last three words. The scar on her head pounded as her mind presented her with terrible scenarios. Josh was dead. Nausea rose in her throat. Her mother was dead. Pain seared across her forehead.

Richard took her hand. "We wanted to tell you before you arrived home. Your house has been burgled."

23

Three times Richard pulled over on the way home for Lizzie to be sick. Her apologies were waved away and cool water provided for her to sip. Rowan whimpered on Sam's shoulder and he soothed her and gave her tissues.

She and Rowan sat holding each other on Richard's sofa while he ran a bath and Sam found a duvet and pillows for the spare room. Lizzie helped Rowan in the bath, gently sponging her back. Wrapped in a towel on Lizzie's lap, Rowan smelled of honeysuckle and clung like a baby koala.

Once she was tucked up, Lizzie ran a little more hot water and allowed her tears to make bore holes in the bubbles. A gentle tap sounded on the door.

"Yes?"

"I was…would you mind not locking the door? I won't…"

"You can come in, Richard."

"I didn't mean…"

"I'm covered in bubbles. Please."

Richard sat cross legged beside the bath.

"You deserve an explanation."

"It can wait."

"No, you do. Did you get my postcard?"

"No, sorry."

"My ex-husband was at Marsha's. She'd invited both of us."

"Ah, well, I guessed he was there. Rowan said...he behaved very badly?"

Lizzie nodded. "The worst he could be but..." More tears fell and she lay back in her bath of iceberg bubbles.

"She said he wasn't her father anymore, that he'd lost the right."

"Sounds reasonable but she doesn't...Could you pass me a towel, please?"

Richard leapt up, grabbed the towel off the heated rail and attempted to pass it to Lizzie while keeping his back to her. Even with her skull constraining a tornado, Lizzie's lips twitched into a smile at his kindness.

"All decent."

In the mirror, she caught a glimpse of a red faced woman with hair on top of her head like an electrocuted pineapple.

"I'm wide awake now, after that coffee. Let me find a robe or something and I can fill you in."

"You sure you don't want to leave it until the morning?"

"I'd...I'd like to tell someone."

"Okay."

"Actually, Richard. I really want to tell you."

The blush scurried across his face. "Don't go rummaging through your bags with Rowan asleep. I've a robe you can borrow. I'll get it."

The lilac light of dawn tinged the sky as Lizzie and Richard huddled together on the sofa. She told him everything. She sensed his curiosity over the photo but he

214

held back, allowing her to finish her story. He held her tightly as she wept for Marsha.

"So it was a holiday of sorts but littered with emotional torment?"

"Seems about right. And now a burglary as well. Plus I'm worried about my mother. Oh, and I'm supposed to be back at work on Monday. Actually, that's tomorrow!"

"Oh, Lizzie." Richard hugged her again and she let him.

Rowan and Sam stirred them, noisily making toast in the kitchen. Lizzie woke first to a pressure on her back and Richard snoring gently behind her. She wriggled from beneath the duvet. Among the pillows and quilt, Richard looked like a cherub resting in the clouds.

She ignored the grinning children in the kitchen and put the kettle on to boil. She grabbed an apple from the fruit bowl.

"You sleep well, Mum?"

Lizzie nodded. "We crashed out after talking into the early hours. My head hurts. Still can't think straight."

"There's filtered water in the jug in the fridge. You're dehydrated, Mrs M."

"Thanks, Sam." She helped herself. "Anyone else?"

"I'm good. What are we going to do, Mum? Sam says the house is safe now. Richard changed all the locks and had the broken window fixed but the police wouldn't let him clear up."

"Dad said they want to know what's missing."

"It's going to be hard to tell though. 'Morning."

Richard stood in the doorway, shifting from foot to foot.

"Would you come to the house with me?"

"Of course."

"I want to come, Mum. You won't know what stuff of mine is missing."

"Okay. Do we need to contact the police first?"

Richard shook his head. "I pulled a few favours. I'll make a list of what's missing and take it to the station. They've dusted for prints but the break in was clean. The burglars knew what they were doing and maybe, what they were looking for."

Lizzie sipped her jasmine tea in the garden. Music flowed through Rowan's open window and Lizzie heard her laugh.

"She sounds better," said Richard.

Lizzie nodded.

"And you're sure? The only things missing are the photos from your bedside and your contract from work?"

"They must know I've been working for you. I'm in danger. Rowan's in danger."

"No, I wouldn't allow that."

"But we are, Richard. Edward Brown had my house burgled because he knows I'm helping you."

"I'm sorry I involved you. I had no idea they would link us together."

"Maybe they haven't but who else would want my contract and family photos? Looks like I'm the next one to be blackmailed."

"I'm so sorry."

"I sound so mean but I'm not having a go. You've done so much and if you hadn't come to feed the chickens, I might have come home to this but getting involved with the Browns has…Richard, is Edward Brown still married?"

"I believe he and his wife have an open marriage."

Lizzie delved through the spare room of her mind. If only she'd had time to use the filing cabinet in there. Under the bed, in a dust covered box, she found it.

"Edward Brown's wife is called Anita."

"How did you know?"

"I met her in Spain. Richard, I have to visit my mother."

She needed him with her but her mother was often condescending to strangers. Lizzie was surprised and delighted how Richard used his charm.

"It's so kind of you to come with Elizabeth. I so rarely have the opportunity to meet her friends."

"I'm pleased to meet you and glad to see you looking so well. Lizzie's been so worried."

"Has she? I told her not to. They were routine tests. Something to do with my liver."

"And the new doctor suggested them?"

"That's right. Dr Warrington, Giles Warrington."

"Is that the new private practise on the high street?"

"Oh no! Dr Warrington is from London."

"He must have come highly recommended for you to travel all that way."

"He comes to me. Such a nice man. Much more understanding than Dr Houghton."

Richard nodded and sipped his tea. Lizzie had never seen a little finger extended so far.

"It's all about trust. Professions providing a service to the public rely on it."

"Most definitely! Doreen trusts Dr Warrington and so do I. She'd rather fly from Spain than see a *foreign* doctor!"

"I don't know a Doreen, Mum."

"Before your time, Elizabeth."

"And you can always trust an old friend, Mrs McCartney."

Patricia McCartney leaned forward from her chair in the conservatory and Richard did the same. "Sometimes it's difficult to know who to trust, Mr Parker. So many secrets and lies."

"I know them well from my profession. Lies compound until there's a web of them, tying people up and choking them and the hardest kept secrets often cause the most harm."

Patricia McCartney sat back, her mouth prim and tight.

"She put you up to this."

"I beg your pardon?"

"Elizabeth McCartney, you're a wicked girl!"

By the time she and Richard returned, Sam and Rowan had tidied the kitchen and found pizza in the freezer. While it cooked, Lizzie moved the heaps of clothes and boxes from her bed into a pile under the window, salvaging two dresses with matching jackets that, with a press with a damp cloth, would get her through two days at work. Hung in her wardrobe with shoes and bags beneath them, Lizzie flopped down onto the bed.

"I'd say you're not seeing my room at its best but truthfully, it was a tip anyway."

"Then don't put it back. Come to mine this week and we'll put a coat of paint on here this weekend."

"Thank you, but I need to be here. Be lovely if you don't mind having Rowan for a bit though."

"Be my pleasure. Sorry I couldn't get further with your mum."

"She's not easy to fool, which is a joke as I'm sure this new doctor isn't who he seems."

"Any evidence?"

"The opposite. Rowan can't find a trace of him online."

Finally, they left, Sam thrilled with his t-shirt and Richard bemused but intrigued with his deer skin frame drum. Lizzie walked from room to room, a ghost in her own house. Defiled and ransacked, it didn't feel like home anymore. An involuntary cry rose from her lips and she ran to her cabin at the bottom of the garden.

The scent of wood and patchouli greeted her and cool air slapped her in the face. She dropped to her knees in her undisturbed Sanctuary. Emotion pounded her, rolling and tumbling her over the floor until she sat cross legged before her altar.

She stilled her breathing, allowing her body to find its rhythm, retuning her with the earth. She lit the candle in the arms of the goddess and from a small drawer, unwrapped a lapis lazuli eight pointed star. Clasped in her hands, Lizzie called down the goddess Ishtar, one of the greatest goddesses of the Middle East but it was one aspect of her in particular Lizzie sought.

> *"Light of the world, goddess of goddesses*
> *Torch of heaven and earth,*
> *Bestower of strength*
> *Hear my prayer.*
>
> *Great Hanata*
> *Give me the power*
> *To face my enemies*
> *With truth on my side.*
>
> *Great goddess, Ishtar*
> *Goddess of love and war*
> *Bathe me in your healing light*
> *Hear my prayer.*
>
> *Mighty Ishtar*
> *Warrior goddess*
> *Fill me with light*
> *So I may face the world."*

Within the confines of the wooden shed, Lizzie allowed the goddess' power to wash over her. Courage, guidance and love coursed through her, heat bursting from her fingertips. From the warrior goddess, she drew protection and imagined herself triumphant in the face of her enemies, not all-conquering but empowered to stand up for what she believed to be right.

24

She was summoned to Edward Brown's office by a message flashing on her computer screen. She stood in front of the mirror in the ladies for more than five minutes, regulating her breathing and summoning her courage. She knew Edward Brown had violated her home, or more likely had sent someone else to do it. She didn't know why he had stolen the contract or her photos but she knew her father and Edward Brown were connected. His face, and her mother's, within a montage of faces also containing Brown's, was proof enough for her.

With the goddess Ishtar with her, Lizzie walked confidently into Edward Brown's office. Brief pleasantries over, Edward Brown placed her contract in front of her and handed her a pen.Lizzie laid the pen on the desk and sat back in her chair.

"I don't think you've been honest with me."

"Then sign the contract and I'll tell you anything you want to know."

It was a clever ploy. Lizzie's fingers itched to pick up the pen.

"How well did you know my father?"

"Why would I know your father, Mrs Martin?"

"I don't know, Mr Brown, but I'm not signing anything until I find out the truth."

"Then you are no longer employed by this company. Pack your desk and leave. HR will send you a letter with details of your final pay."

Lizzie rose slowly from her chair, held back by the weighty chains of fear.

"Shame you'll lose your pretty house."

Edward's final words were the catalyst she needed. Like a dragon from its lair, Lizzie unfurled.

"I'm not losing anything, Mr Brown. You can trash my house and steal my photos but you'll not manipulate me like you did my father!"

She ran down the corridor, phoning Richard from her mobile. He would drop Rowan and Sam off at the police station and collect her from under the oak tree in the park.

She sat beneath the leafy boughs, her back pressed against the ancient trunk. The pain in her head eased, a warm sensation travelling up her spine, linking her heart beat to the rise and fall of energy within the tree. Pictures rose up in her mind behind her closed eyelids. Tension left her body, taken away by the tree and replaced with clarity of mind. She remembered the cool smooth surface of the quartz crystal and opened her third eye.

She walked up the steps to the party. She was introduced by Marsha, along the receiving line. She saw all the men and Doreen Klein, flushed with alcohol and her head in the clouds but there was something else. The fear in Doreen's eyes. What did Doreen know? *Doreen?* Oh no!

They raced to her mother's house, Richard making calls on his hands free as they drove. She cursed the traffic and swore at the traffic lights. A sleek black car was parked outside her mother's house. They ran through the back door, Lizzie calling out as they flew up the stairs. Richard pushed past her into her mother's room, knocking the doctor and his syringe against the wall. With practised constraint, he spun Dr Warrington around, and snapped on handcuffs.

Lizzie held her mother as she screamed.

"You're okay, mum. Everything's going to be okay."

"You stupid girl! I want to end it like this! I'll not fester in a hospital the rest of my life!"

"Mum, there's nothing wrong with you."

"Of course there is!"

Lizzie slapped her mother's face. Patricia McCartney sat back on her pillows, wide eyed with shock.

"You have to listen! That man is not a real doctor. Do you hear me? Doreen told you about him, remember! Klein, Anders, Masters, Bergen, all of them! They set you up!"

Patricia McCartney's eyes resembled saucers.

"You wouldn't tell me about the past, about Dad, about Simon and Aunt Eleanor or your visit to Spain, and it nearly got you killed! You have to tell me what happened!"

Defiance settled on Patricia McCartney's face. She folded her arms.

"Our house was broken into while we were away and I've been threatened at work. We have to put a stop to this. Rowan's in danger."

She spoke the final words without thinking and they were the ones to sway her mother's resolve.

Patricia McCartney nodded briefly before weeping into her hands.

Richard took charge when the police arrived, leaving Lizzie alone with her mother.

Mrs McCartney remained in bed, sipping tea from her favourite china cup while Lizzie sat on the bed. She handed Lizzie her empty cup.

"I made a promise, Elizabeth and I don't like breaking it."

"But you'll do anything to protect Rowan."

Her mother nodded.

"I met your father at a Jubilee Party in London, or rather we met him, your Aunt Eleanor and I. There were hundreds of people there. Including Edward Brown, your father's employer."

"I guessed as much. Go on."

"I'd spent my life nursing your grandparents and suddenly, I was free. Your father introduced us. Edward was charming, debonair and rich and I was his dance partner for the whole evening. While your father and Eleanor, who were much closer in age, threw themselves into the common dances, reels and such like, Edward and I talked. He was eloquent and well-read and we enjoyed a number of pleasant evenings together."

"Edward Brown? You and Edward Brown?"

Her mother nodded. "Your father...Your father loved Eleanor."

Lizzie slid off the eiderdown and landed on the floor. "Go on."

"You looked for Eleanor, didn't you?"

"Yes, mother but tell me about Edward."

"He…We…let's say, the relationship ended, for him anyway."

Lizzie crawled onto her knees, her chin on her arms on the bed. "But you were pregnant."

"I was alone and scared."

"You had Eleanor."

Fury raged in Patricia McCartney's eyes. "That changeling! She was my adopted sister, delivered to our door to make my life hell!"

"Adopted!"

"My parents believed I required a sibling and they were unable to produce one. I was five years old when a noisy toddler entered my life and called me sister. I hated her from the moment I saw her!"

"While Dad… why? Why did Dad marry you?"

"Because Edward Brown told him to."

"Wait…Edward needed you married off. You pestered him, didn't you?"

"I loved him! He was the father of my son!"

"So they swapped babies so Brown could be near Simon while Eleanor's baby, you, were brought up by Granny McCartney and Dad! Granny's not your Mum!"

"I know."

Lizzie and Rowan sat on garden chairs in Richard's garden, the men on the far side lighting the barbeque, giving the women some privacy.

"But why did…why did Granddad…"

"Granny McCartney was jealous of his relationship with me. I knew that but not why, until now. She didn't want his love or mine but she didn't want us to have each other either. Her child had been taken from her then he died. On top of that, she'd been rejected by the man she loved. Granddad turned to drink when she blackmailed him into keeping away from me. I still don't know exactly how he died. Richard gave me an outline of what the police discovered."

"And?"

"It fits in with a vision I had after I hit my head in the bar. He was drunk. He was on a bridge. Then he was gone. It might have been suicide or maybe he fell. We'll never know."

"And you still don't remember why you fainted in the bar?"

Lizzie shook her head. "I have no idea. I remember being at work that day, the dream of the man jumping from the bridge and then I woke up in hospital. It hurts when I try and search for more."

"Don't then." Rowan sighed. "She's not my Granny anymore."

Rowan's sad face pulled at Lizzie's heart. "It seems to me, it's not so much in the title as the action, don't you think? Granny has always treated you as her granddaughter. I don't think that should change, do you?"

"You forgive her?"

"It wasn't her doing, Rowan. She was used by Edward Brown, same as Granddad."

"I'd like to talk to her, maybe with Sam."

"I think you should. She'll listen to you."

The chilled rosé tickled her nose. It was her second glass but with no work tomorrow, or in the foreseeable future, she didn't care.

"They've made the Spanish arrests. You were right about Coleman. With protection, he'll tell all he knows," said Richard.

"He's obeyed his father then the Browns all his life. I hope this works out well for Errol and he gets the protection he needs."

"Good looking man, is he?"

Lizzie winked at Richard. "Hell yeah!"

Devastation flickered across Richard's face before smiling benevolence resumed. Lizzie grabbed his hands.

"I'm teasing you, Richard. He's closer to Rowan's age than mine!"

Richard looked at his hands. "I wouldn't blame you. You are single."

"And right now, I'm happy to stay that way. You said before we went away, about needing to straighten yourself out. I've found out after thirty eight years that my mother isn't my mother, my father worked for a bunch of gangsters, I only got my job because they wanted to keep an eye on me and my real mother is alive and living in

Wales somewhere. I could certainly do with some straightening out!"

"That's a lot for one person. How're you feeling, apart from confused?"

Lizzie sat back and sipped at her drink. "Surprisingly good. Not sure how I'm going to pay the mortgage next month but I've made a decision about one thing."

"Which is?"

"The next job I interview for, I'll be sure to check before I start that I can wear what I like!"

Acknowledgements

Thank you Peter Jones, writer, cover designer supreme, formatting hero and true friend.

Thank you first readers, especially Melanie Collier and Mel Jackson Bridge, for your valuable feedback.

Thank you friends and fellow authors on social media for your help and support.

And the final thank you to Mike, my partner, my love, for allowing me to read aloud and share the workings of my mind as this first Witch Lit novel took shape.

Printed in Great Britain
by Amazon